Death at the Harbour Arms

Veronica Vale Investigates - book 5

Kitty Kildare

K.E. O'Connor Books

Copyright © 2024 by Kitty Kildare

All rights reserved. No part of this publication may be reproduced, distributed, or transmitted in any form or by any means, including photocopying, recording, or other electronic or mechanical methods, without the prior written permission of the publisher, except as permitted by U.S. copyright law.

For permission requests, contact: kittykildare@kittykildare.com

The story, all names, characters, and incidents portrayed in this production are fictitious. No identification with actual persons (living or deceased), places, buildings, and products is intended or should be inferred.

DEATH AT THE HARBOUR ARMS

ISBN: 978-1-915378-85-9

Book Cover by Victoria Cooper

Chapter 1

"Benji! Come back here this instant." I stood with my hands on my hips as he ignored me, bounding towards the water's edge.

"Let him play. He's enjoying himself," Jacob Templeton muttered.

I glanced at the reason we were on a beach in Margate, Kent. Jacob sat in a striped deckchair, not looking a jot happy to be on this glorious beach with the sun shining and the seagulls screaming as they dive bombed people to snatch their ice creams. But I'd ferried him to this pretty seaside town for some much-needed rest and recovery after a near-fatal incident with an unexploded bomb, so here he was going to stay.

"Benji never misbehaves," I said. "Something must be amiss. Hold on a moment. There's somebody flailing about in the waves. Oh! Good boy! Benji's off to rescue them."

By now, several people had gathered at the water's edge as Benji ploughed through the waves, doggy paddling towards the unfortunate swimmer who'd got themselves into trouble.

Ruby Smythe stood and joined me, sporting a daring patterned bathing suit consisting of shorts and a short-sleeved top, made from a fitted fabric. "Isn't that your mother?"

"She'd never go swimming in the sea. Mother spent an hour this very morning telling me about the swim tents they used to protect a lady's modesty. She's paddling in the shallows over there." I pointed to the spot where I'd last seen my usually bedbound mother, dipping her toes into the chilly waters. It was a rare occasion the sea in this country went above skin achingly cool, and despite several weeks of sunshine, only the hardiest ventured into the water any deeper than an ankle.

"I don't see her." Ruby shaded her eyes with a hand. "Are you sure that's not Edith having difficulty? She's wearing the same flowered bathing cap."

Benji was almost to the swimmer, kicking up water as he headed towards her and causing the woman to scream even more. That scream did have a familiar ear-splitting pitch.

"Oh, my life! It is her. Whatever is she doing, going so far out?" I took a step forward.

"Edith was telling me over breakfast that she used to enjoy swimming," Ruby said.

"Thirty years ago! She barely gets out of bed these days. She won't have the strength to tackle the waves." I kicked off my shoes.

"What do you think you're doing?" Ruby asked.

"Ensuring my only living parent remains alive. Are you coming with me?"

Ruby wrinkled her adorable nose. "Benji has everything in hand. Or should that be paw? And there are a few strapping chaps following him. Edith may enjoy being escorted back to the beach by those young men as they worry about her wellbeing."

I paused before getting involved in the rescue attempt. Sure enough, several people were assisting my bedraggled mother, her flowered bathing cap now askew, back into safer waters. Although, I realised she'd been in the shallows this whole time. The beach at Margate had a gentle and safe slope out into the deeper waters. You could walk quite some way before needing to swim.

"She must have panicked." Jacob leaned forward in the deckchair. "Or got a cramp. The cold can do that if you're not careful. I'd have helped, but..."

I glanced down at him again. He was under a sunshade, a hat pulled low over his eyes. One leg up to the knee was in full plaster, and he still had a small bandage on his head, which was concealed by the hat. We'd been in Margate for a week, and although most of us were enjoying ourselves, Jacob rarely cracked a smile. And he kept nudging me to have serious conversations about our future. A discussion I wasn't ready to tackle. A woman needed a plan in place before attempting such tricky business.

"You'll soon be strong enough to rescue any damsel who finds herself in trouble." I waved to my mother, so she could get her bearings and knew where to direct her heroes as they carried her between them, Benji close behind, soggy, but wagging his tail.

"That could take months. I'm healing too slowly," Jacob grumbled.

"That's enough of the surly talk," Ruby said. "I know what'll cheer you up. I'll get ice creams for all of us. Your mother will need something sweet to get over the shock of almost drowning."

"She was barely in up to her waist," I muttered. My mother's flare for the dramatics was the stuff of legends.

"None for me. I'll just get sand in it," Jacob said.

"Don't be such a grump," Ruby said. "Jacob, you must cheer up!"

"It's Inspector—" Jacob sighed, cutting himself off. "Sorry. I keep forgetting I'm no longer of service to people."

Ruby looked at me and raised her eyebrows. This was the cause of his consternation. Just before Jacob had been sent home from the hospital, his superior had written to him saying he was no longer fit for service and had been discharged from the police. Of course, since he received his injury during active duty, he'd receive a full pension and dispensation benefits, but Jacob didn't want that. He was a man of service who desired to help others. He'd always pursued the path of justice, so it was a bitter blow to have everything taken away in that single, thoughtless letter written by his fool of an employer.

When I'd suggested a restorative trip to the seaside, I'd intended it to be light-hearted and relaxing. And I'd been thrilled when my mother and Matthew had agreed to come with us. Although it had taken weeks of discussion and several changes of mind before the plan was enacted. Now, I just needed to get Jacob smiling more and no one else attempting to drown, and everything would be perfect.

"Oh my! Did you see what happened to me? I should never have left my bed." My mother, Edith Vale, staggered over, suitably assisted by two men in fitted swim suits. "I went under the waves three times. I lost my footing and then couldn't catch my breath. I thought I was a goner."

Benji stood beside my mother, wagging his tail, happy she wasn't dead.

"How deep was the water?" I asked.

"Deep enough! I feared the worst. And there was something beneath the water. It brushed my leg."

"There are jelly fish in the sea," Ruby said, her blue eyes wide. "Did you get stung?"

"Don't encourage her," I muttered. "Thank you, gentlemen. I'll look after her from here."

"Let me give you something for your troubles." My mother reached for her handbag, but the gentlemen kindly declined and slid away.

"I was getting us all ice creams," Ruby said. "Edith, I'll get you an extra scoop, shall I? You can celebrate not drowning."

"I'm not sure I could eat. My heart is racing. Matthew, feel my pulse."

My unfortunate brother, Matthew, had been lumbered with being our mother's unofficial nurse while on this trip. I hadn't anticipated that would happen, but she only felt comfortable when she was checked on at least once an hour and always had somebody by her side. Matthew had his own troubles, but our mother's health preoccupations had kept him busy and the worst of his post-war tremors and trials at bay.

Matthew's unamused gaze met mine as he held out a hand for my mother's wrist. She tumbled into the deckchair beside him, twittering and spluttering, until he told her to be quiet or he wouldn't be able to get an accurate reading and would assume she was about to perish.

"Go and get those ice creams," I whispered to Ruby. "Once Mother's eaten, she'll forget about almost drowning."

Ruby paid me no attention, her gaze fixed on two tanned, dark-haired men strutting along the beach, each wearing fitted swim suits. I had no idea they made such revealing gentlemen's beach attire.

"The ice creams!" I nudged her hard in the ribs with an elbow.

Ruby jumped. "Yes! I'll take the scenic route." She grabbed her handbag.

"Is the scenic route following those nearly naked men?" I asked.

"Aren't they handsome?" Ruby reapplied her lipstick. "I've seen them on the beach every day since we've been here. They're excellent swimmers. And no sign of any lady friends. I overheard them speaking, not in English. I believe they're Italian. It's such an attractive language."

"Have you inspected for rings on fingers?" I couldn't hide my smile. Ruby was a perpetual romantic, no matter how many times her heart was bruised.

"A lack of a ring isn't a clear sign of availability. It's unlikely they'd wear jewellery on the beach in case they lost it. But from what I've seen, no rings and no tan lines either, so they could be single. We could have one each." Ruby's gaze cut to Jacob. "Unless you're otherwise engaged."

I risked a cheeky smile at Jacob. "I do need to brush up on my Italian."

Ruby tittered. "Shall I see if they're available?"

"Just the ice cream for me," I said.

Ruby dashed off, going in the opposite direction of the café selling ice cream. We'd be lucky if we saw any sweet treats today.

Jacob sighed as I settled back next to him.

"I was only teasing about the Italians," I said. "Besides, I've never had a talent for languages, and you know I enjoy a jolly good conversation."

"I wouldn't blame you." His gaze was on the sea.

"For what? Chasing after an Italian holiday romance?"

Jacob was quiet for a moment. "For wanting something more."

"I have everything I need right here. But if you're having such a bad time, we can go home early," I murmured, making sure my mother and Matthew didn't hear. "Is it the hotel? It's not five-star, but it's close to the Harbour Arms." This holiday served three purposes: one, to ensure Jacob got the rest he required. Two, to ensure I could investigate the pubs we owned. Although my late father purchased pubs mainly in London and the surrounding towns and villages, he sometimes had a fancy for travelling farther, which is how we came to be in Kent. And three, to consider expanding my expertise into a new area.

"The hotel is fine." Jacob shifted in his deckchair. "Sorry. I don't mean to be so surly. It's my leg. It troubled me all night, and I can't seem to get comfortable."

I was instantly on the alert. "Have you checked for any infection? Does it feel hot?"

"No, but it's not healing as fast as I need it to."

"It's healing at exactly the right speed," I said. "It may not be fast enough for you, but you can't rush these things. If you push too hard, you'll relapse and end up back in the hospital. Are you taking all your medication?"

"I hate those pills. They make me sleepy."

I tapped his arm. "So, no medication all day? We've had breakfast and been for a long walk. It's no wonder your leg is protesting. Get rid of that male mulishness and take your pills."

Jacob grumbled about me being too stubborn for my own good.

I replied with a most unladylike snort. "I may be stubborn, but I'm no fool. You'll feel pain if you're not taking the prescribed medication."

"I get a rash on my chest when I take them," Jacob said.

"A rash or a crippling pain? I know which I'd choose. You can always cover up if you're self-conscious about your rash." I glanced at Jacob's white linen shirt with two buttons undone. He wore long shorts and a pair of slip-on shoes, clothing I'd picked to be practical on the beach and easy for him to manage with one leg in plaster without the need for me to fuss too much.

"I don't mean to spoil the day," Jacob said quietly. "I'll go back to the hotel and take my pills."

"You'll do no such thing. I have them right here." I opened my handbag, dispensed two pills, and handed them to him.

He stared at me agog. "How did you know?"

"I've been around you long enough to realise you'll put on a brave face when there's no need. And... I may have counted the number of pills in your bottle yesterday when I checked on you before we went down to breakfast."

"And you snuck back into my room and pinched them?"

"No! I borrowed them for your own good in case you needed them," I said.

There was more muttering, but he took the pills, so the pain must have been bad.

I turned to my mother. "Are you feeling better after your bracing swim?"

"Don't joke about such a thing," she said. "My heart still hasn't settled into its proper rhythm, has it, Matthew?"

Matthew was huddled under a large towel. It was where he spent most of his time when we were on the beach. I didn't mind him swaddling himself for comfort. I was simply delighted he'd left the family home. There had been plenty of wobbles on the journey down from London, when he'd kept changing his mind and saying it was too much for Felix, his new dog, but he'd braved it out. And other than the need to retreat under a large towel from time to time, he seemed less distressed.

I hoped that meant we'd turned a corner. Matthew worried me ever so much when he'd become a hermit, refusing to leave the house, or sometimes even talk to me.

I turned my face to the sun and inhaled deeply. The sea air and the sunshine really were miraculous cures.

I called Benji over, fed him a small treat, and rubbed him down with a towel, which he thoroughly enjoyed. "You're such a brave dog. Well done for spotting the trouble."

"He's our hero dog," my mother said.

"I'm glad you think so. I may need to leave him with you while I look at more offices. Not everywhere in this town is dog-friendly," I said.

My mother tutted and shook her head. "I still don't understand this private investigation nonsense. I don't want any daughter of mine running around chasing criminals."

Jacob chuckled softly out of my mother's earshot. "She's not aware of your hobbies?"

"I tell her everything, and she adores the gory details of all the cases. But Mother worries for my safety," I whispered.

"She's not the only one," he said.

"Mrs Vale! What a delight to find you here." Colonel Basil Griffin appeared in front of us. He was retired, in his late sixties, and sported a dapper handlebar moustache, which was as white as the thick hair on his head. The man was blind in one eye, but it didn't slow him. Ever since we'd arrived at our hotel, he'd taken a shine to my mother and kept turning up everywhere we were, insisting on escorting her places. Of course, my mother protested and said she didn't want any man's attentions, but the way she blushed and flustered belied her true feelings.

"Colonel Griffin," my mother said. "I'm embarrassed for you to see me in this bedraggled state. Did you know I almost drowned?"

"My dear lady, perish the thought," he said. "You need a restorative drink after such a drama. Allow me to escort you to the Golden Lounge. It's the most prestigious venue in Margate and a short stroll from here. They do a delicious gin fizz."

"I couldn't. And that's more Veronica's drink than mine," my mother said.

Colonel Griffin addressed me with a nod.

"My mother adores sherry or champagne," I said. "Does the Golden Lounge serve either of those drinks?"

"Veronica!" my mother hissed at me.

"Of course! And by the time we get there, it will be past noon, so an acceptable hour for a bracing drink. Please, I'd be honoured if you'd accompany a lonely old warrior. I promise, I'll be on my best behaviour and only bore you with a few stories."

"I shouldn't leave Matthew," my mother said, even though there was a hopeful glint in her eyes.

"I'm fine," he muttered from beneath his towel.

"Enjoy yourself," I said. "We're not leaving the beach for another two hours. That gives you plenty of time to catch up with your new friend."

"If you're sure." My mother was already gathering things together, while Colonel Griffin held out his elbow for her to take.

We watched in silence as my allegedly frail mother walked confidently along the sand with her new companion.

Jacob cleared his throat. "Veronica, there's something I want to discuss with you."

I grimaced. Here we go again. He'd suggested discussing 'something' several times since we'd arrived in Margate, and each time, I'd brushed him off. I knew what Jacob wanted to talk about. I'd expressed feelings towards him, and there'd been a small kiss. I'd avoided discussing both things, mainly because I didn't have any solution.

"If you're concerned about the offices we're looking at, you only need to say," I said briskly. "There are plenty of options. We'll keep searching until we find the right one."

"That's not what I'm interested in talking about," Jacob said. "Although I'm not sure it's a practical business, but I'm willing to listen. It's about—"

"Good. Then there's nothing else to discuss. Not right now. We're here to enjoy ourselves and ensure you recover."

"But I really want to—"

"No, no. I insist on silence. Don't you have that new book you want to read?" I despised cutting people off, but my ears would go pink with embarrassment if Jacob brought up the subject of romance.

He sighed. "You're really serious about opening your own private investigation business here?"

"I couldn't be more serious," I said, glad the topic of conversation had shifted. "You have the makings of an excellent private investigator, and so do I. No more serious talk. Sand, sea, and sunbathing. That's all we should focus on."

From his disgruntled sigh, I realised I'd won that battle, but not yet the war.

Chapter 2

"I can understand Jacob's reticence about relocating here." Ruby slid her foot into a low-heeled T-strap shoe as she sat on the side of her bed in our shared hotel room. "I never really thought about it until we were actually here. Margate is a long way from home."

I tidied my windswept hair and put on my own shoes. They were flatter than Ruby's and a practical brown. "You said it was a fun journey."

"And it was! Don't think I'm complaining. Since we've been in Margate, I've had a tremendous time," Ruby replied.

"You don't like the private investigation idea?" I asked. "It's not so different from what we've been doing with the police. And at least I'll get paid."

"I never thought you'd give up your job as a journalist," Ruby said. "You worked hard to get your position. Your Uncle Harry will miss you terribly."

"That's something I haven't told you," I said. "Uncle Harry wants to set up regional branches for the newspaper. He thinks there are opportunities to have a more local flavour to the news. While I'm here looking at offices for my private investigation firm, I'm keeping an eye out for suitable premises for him."

"Oh! I suppose that is a good idea," Ruby said. "Will you divide your time between the two roles?"

"I've yet to decide." I sat beside her on the single bed. We were sharing a room in the hotel. My mother and Matthew were next door, and Jacob had his own room next to theirs. "What's wrong, old bean? I can always tell when something is on your mind."

Ruby huffed out a small sigh. "What will I do when you leave London?"

"What makes you think I'm leaving London?"

"You have these big plans for Kent. Your own investigation business with Jacob. Setting up a regional newspaper office for your Uncle Harry. You'll be too busy for me."

"You absolute ninny." I gently swatted her knee. "London will always be my home. It needs to be, since I'll never be able to convince Matthew or my mother to leave. Besides, I adore living there. I occasionally complain about the hustle and bustle, but the convenience more than makes up for it. You can get everything you require in one place."

"There may be towns like that in Kent that persuade you to remain here," Ruby said. "I know it's silly, but I always imagined us growing old together. We'd be disreputable older ladies. You'd have several dozen dogs, and I'd have an entourage of younger men to pay me attention. We'd live in a crumbling house close to the shops, so we had everything we needed. And of course, there'd be a big green space for you to walk your dogs."

"That's a marvellous dream, and one you should cling to. I thoroughly support it." I put an arm around Ruby's shoulders and hugged her. "I'm staying right where I am. And here's the final piece of my grand plan. Jacob is to have an office and a base here while I remain in London."

Ruby gasped. "What does he think about that?"

"We've yet to discuss it, but couples work best when they aren't in each other's pockets," I said. "After all, if you never spend at least a day apart, what do you talk about around the dinner table?"

"Couple?" Ruby squeaked. "You finally admit you want to be with him?"

"I admit to nothing." I smiled gently. "But I am fond of Jacob, and he knows it now. This can't be rushed, though. We're both used to our own company and doing things our own way."

Ruby pursed her lips. "That doesn't sound romantic."

"Romance is over-rated. I thought Jacob could have a useful purpose in Kent, and I could pop down at the weekends. Maybe come for the holidays, or if he has a particularly difficult case, I'd join him, and we could figure things out together."

"Practical as ever."

"It's worked so far."

"You're so good to him," Ruby said. "Most women would abandon a man when he becomes injured and loses his fortune."

"Jacob is healing, and he's far from lost his fortune," I said. "He will receive a good pension from the police. And so he should. If he hadn't been working for them, he wouldn't have been injured by that bomb."

"You promise you won't abandon me in London?" Ruby asked. "I have no other friends."

"Absolute lies!" Ruby could talk to anyone. "I may not be able to promise I'll stay in London forever, but I assure you, I have no plans to go anywhere for a long time."

Ruby's expression brightened. "Then I'm not unhappy. This is an ideal spot for a holiday. I thoroughly support this idea. It's excellent."

"Don't get too excited," I said. "I need to sell it to Jacob. He may not want to leave London."

"He will. I can tell he's done with London," Ruby said. "His time in the police was jading him, and his surliness was becoming unacceptable. And after the foul treatment by his fool of a boss, he'll be glad to try something new. Especially if it means he gets to spend more time with you."

"At the weekends only. I'm taking it one step at a time," I said. "We need to find the perfect office first, and then I'll convince Jacob it's the right thing for both of us."

"If anyone can do it, you can." Ruby checked the time. "We must hurry. We don't want to be late for dinner."

"You must be hungry if you plan to arrive on time. And after all the ice cream you ate, I'm surprised you have room for dinner." I collected my handbag and Benji, and we left our room.

"What makes you think I ate a lot of ice cream today?" Ruby asked.

"You were gone from the beach for over two hours," I said. "And when you returned with our ice creams, you couldn't stop beaming. I assumed…" I trailed off, not hiding my smile.

Ruby tittered behind one hand. "I got talking and lost track of time. Those two Italian men were so charming."

"I thought as much. I hope they didn't charm you too much; otherwise, I won't see you for the rest of the holiday."

"You'll see plenty of me. They're busy working. They're performing at the new amusements."

"I've been hearing all about the Margate attractions," I said.

"I thought we might visit this evening." Ruby slid me a glance. "My new Italian friends will be there."

"We? I hope you haven't arranged a double date."

"No! But I said we'd like to look at the rides and the new entertainment venue. If we just so happen to bump into Ricardo and Alfonso..."

"Already on first-name terms?"

Ruby shrugged. "When there are so few eligible men around, a lady must move with great haste. You will come with me, won't you? Italian men are very... strident in their interests."

"I'm sure we'll all enjoy a visit to the amusements after dinner," I said.

We met my mother, Jacob, and a nervous Matthew in the hotel lobby. Ruby instantly caught hold of Matthew's arm. "You must look after me this evening. Your sister is concerned I'm turning into a wayward woman."

"We're a little past that point," I murmured.

Matthew gripped Felix's lead and nodded. He was always at the peak of his nerves just before we embarked on an adventure. Once he was immersed in the activities, he relaxed, but this was the danger zone.

At any second, he could flee to his room and we wouldn't see him all evening.

"We're going to the Harbour Arms for dinner," I announced. "It's a short walk along the promenade. Plenty of space and fresh air, and not too many people."

Matthew relaxed a fraction at that good news.

"And they do a marvellous fish and chip supper." It was one of Matthew's favourite treats.

"All the fresh air has made me hungry," my mother said. "Although my feet are troubling me something terrible. We'll need to take it slowly."

"Allow me to escort you." Jacob held out his elbow for my mother to take.

She grabbed it and smiled. "Such a gentleman. I don't want to be any bother to you, though. I won't be too much for your leg?"

"Thanks to Veronica reminding me about my medication, I'm feeling as bright as a button." Jacob gestured to the door. "Shall we?"

We stepped out of the hotel, which was located on the Margate seafront. The tide was out, revealing a vast expanse of damp sand. The air was sharp and fresh and already cooling as the sun slowly dipped. But I was warm enough in my dropped waist blue dress with a lightweight beaded shawl.

"Veronica! Wait. I'm glad I caught you."

I turned towards the familiar female voice and smiled as Emily Brewer approached me. She was several years my junior, bright and determined, and forging a journalistic path. Her dark hair was cut into a fashionable style, and she wore trousers and a tailored shirt. It was a masculine look, but it suited her.

"Emily! I thought we'd arranged to meet at the Harbour Arms?" We briefly exchanged kisses.

"I'm running late. Aunt Mabel will have my guts for garters. But I have a lead on a new story, and I had to investigate."

"Good for you. Any luck?" We walked behind the others, Benji trotting beside me.

"It's early days, but I'm excited. In fact, I've been working on several stories. I'd love to talk them through with you this evening if we have a moment."

"I'm always happy to exchange ideas." I didn't know Emily well, although our paths had crossed a dozen times. Her aunt, Mabel Fletcher, had run the Harbour Arms for five years. When Emily's parents died, Mabel took her in, and she'd been living above the pub ever since.

"What have you got planned for tonight?" Emily asked.

"Ruby is all set on visiting the amusements."

"There's so much to do here," Emily said. "If dancing is your thing, they've just opened a new ballroom. And there's the scenic railway ride."

I studied Jacob's steady limp. "Dancing may not be on the cards, but we'll enjoy a ride on the railway."

"It'll be busy. You'll have to queue. But it'll be worth it," Emily said. "I even got a free ride because I wrote an article for the local newspaper to encourage people to try it."

"I'm glad you mentioned newspapers," I said. "My Uncle Harry is considering opening a branch of the London Times down here. Of course, it would be called the Kent Times. We'll be looking for eager journalists to join the team. What do you think?"

Emily's eyes widened and a huge grin lit her pretty face. "Count me in. Of course, I want to write real stories. I'm happy to write pieces for the tourists about the new amusements. All the visitors are regenerating the area after the war, but I'm researching serious stories. That's where I plan on making my name."

"Tales of corruption and dark deeds, do you mean?"

Emily's expression grew serious. "Absolutely that. We really need to talk."

"Do hurry, Veronica," my mother said.

"We'll find a moment to catch up when there are fewer distractions," I said to Emily.

It was a ten-minute walk to the Harbour Arms. It was an attractive pub overlooking the seafront. Tall, arched windows with decorative mullions lined the front, and a wide entrance sat at the centre of the building. The interior was a warm, welcoming space with dark wooden panelling on the walls, polished oak floors, and a carved wooden bar that ran the length of the main room. Large, framed mirrors and vintage maritime-themed artwork adorned the walls. The scent of fresh sea air mixed with the comforting aroma of hearty pub fare that wafted from the kitchen.

Mabel Fletcher welcomed us in with open arms. She was a robust woman who'd just turned fifty, with a head of messy dark curls and an almost permanent smile on her face. She seated us at one of the best tables by the window with a sea view, and within minutes, we all had huge plates of delicious fish and chips in front of us.

When Mabel had set down the last plate, she stepped back and smiled, settling her hands on her hips. "That'll fuel your fire for an evening of fun."

"I've already been telling them about the ballroom and the railway." Emily walked over with a gin and tonic in her hand.

"What's this about a railway?" Jacob asked.

"It's a scenic railway route. Part of the newly named Dreamland amusements," Mabel said. "It opened to entertain all the tourists we've been getting. There are also the arcades and a circus, which isn't my thing. The seafront rides, too. The Ferris wheel and bumper cars. The children adore those."

"What route does the railway take?" Jacob asked. "How far does it go?"

Mabel chuckled. "Is this your first time visiting Margate?"

He shook his head. "But I haven't been here for years. Veronica insisted on this destination."

"And you can never say no to this lady."

Jacob acknowledged the comment with a raised eyebrow.

"It's less scenic than you may think." Emily smiled at her aunt. "It's a rollercoaster!"

My mother dropped her fork. "I wouldn't survive such an adventure."

"It's safe," Mabel said. "It's only recently opened, so everything is new. And they have a chap who rides with you to control the speed. If you go too fast, he applies the brakes."

"Although lots of riders call out to go faster and faster." Emily laughed. "I've been on it."

My mother flapped and fluttered, not convinced.

"Or if you're looking for more adult entertainment," Mabel said, "you should visit one of the new clubs. Tommy McAllister runs most of them. Just be careful which one you go to, or you could end up with a lady sitting in your lap."

"He runs gentlemen's clubs?" Jacob asked.

"Dancing. Drinking. Ladies. A different flavour for everyone. Tommy has his fingers in a lot of pies," Mabel said. "Don't worry. We'll tell you the best places to go. You must hurry with your meals, though. Lady Lizzie Hargreaves is opening the expansion to the seaside amusements this evening. There'll be a ribbon-cutting ceremony and fireworks."

"Lady Lizzie gave me my journalism scholarship," Emily said. "She has a passion for the arts and literature. She's so supportive of the local community."

"That'll be a good place to start," I said. It seemed we were in for an entertaining evening.

After we'd finished our moreish fish and chips, I was so full I could barely move, so I was glad of the fresh air and exercise as we walked towards the newly expanded amusement park. It was quite a sight, with lights flashing and the scent of toffee apples in the air.

Ruby still protected Matthew. She'd kept him under her wing since we'd arrived in Margate, acting like the hopeless damsel to give him more responsibility. But I could tell from the tense set of his shoulders he found the crowds and noise difficult. I'd watch him, and if it became too much, I'd gently suggest he return to the hotel because Felix was overstimulated.

"There's Tommy!" Mabel and Emily had joined us for the opening event, and Mabel pointed out the local businessman. "He's a bad boy, come good. But his past still follows him around."

"He's the chap who operates the gentlemen's clubs?" I asked.

"And some of the amusements. He has the penny slot places as well."

Tommy was a tall man with broad shoulders. He strode through the crowd with purposeful intent, his dark hair slicked back, as was the fashion.

"And here's one of our supposed titans of local business," Mabel said. "That's George Havisham, our councillor. Although he's more interested in going fishing than regeneration. He blows a lot of hot air but gets little done." George was an older gent with wispy hair and a pot belly, shaking hands with various people as he strolled through the crowd in a smart, dark suit.

"Good evening, Mabel. Emily." A short man with a wispy moustache and a warm smile stopped in front of us. "I see you're entertaining guests this evening."

Mabel made the introductions. "This is Doctor Richard Patterson. He's our local doctor."

"For my troubles," Doctor Patterson said. "It's a pleasure to meet you all."

"Could you help me with my aching feet?" My mother bustled closer. "I think it's all the walking we've been doing, but I'm worried I'm developing bunions. I spend most of my time in bed, you see. I have so many health problems and I can't overexert myself."

"If you would like to make an appointment, I can see you early next week." Doctor Patterson stepped back, clearly not wanting to have anything to do with my mother's feet.

"Let's not bother the doctor," I said. "I'll look at your feet this evening. They just need a soak in some Epsom salts and you'll be right as rain."

A group of scantily dressed ladies with feather boas and dramatic makeup strutted past, causing several men to wolf-whistle and the crowd to part.

"Oh my," Ruby said. "Who are they? Part of the circus?"

"That's the burlesque troupe. They were trained by an American dancer. They work for Tommy," Mabel said. "He sends them out to drum up trade for the evening shows. Do you see the one at the front with the red hair? That's Ivy Vance. She's the queen of burlesque. She cuts quite a scene, don't you think?"

They were all stunning women with extraordinary figures. They oozed confidence, and I could tell from their toned physiques that they were professional dancers.

There was a shout for quiet, and the crowd jostled closer together.

"Hurry, hurry." Mabel bustled us along. "The opening ceremony is about to begin." She barged her way through until we were almost at the front. There was a stage set up, upon which stood an elegant lady of around forty in a green silk gown, her hair done in fashionable finger waves.

Her calm gaze took in the crowd until she had everybody's attention. "Good evening, everybody. Welcome to this most enchanting event. The fun is about to begin."

Chapter 3

The crowd was enthralled as Lady Lizzie talked about the new entertainments opening on Margate pier and promenade. It all sounded jolly exciting—more rides, activities for the children, and tea dances for the older crowd. I missed dancing. There were so many dances during the Great War, but since peace arrived in all its glorious fanfare, the basic afternoon and evening dances had taken a backseat.

"Isn't it incredible?" Emily whispered to me. "I couldn't believe it when Lady Lizzie picked my essay out of all the applicants and awarded me a scholarship. I'd be nothing if it weren't for her support."

"You're hard-working and dedicated," I said. "You could have achieved success without her financial aid, but I'm sure it was most welcome."

"I came top of my class," Emily said proudly. "Lady Lizzie was so pleased, and she hosted an afternoon tea at her home, Hartsdown House. All the students she supported attended, along with our families. And Lady Lizzie was so welcoming and interested in our plans for the future."

"This is only the beginning for Margate's glorious growth." Lady Lizzie's cut-glass accent revealed her high-class upbringing. "And I can reveal this evening another exciting part of that expansion. The council has formally approved our new arts centre."

There was a round of applause that went on for a good minute before Lady Lizzie quietened the crowd.

"I'm as excited as all of you. We plan on hosting a series of musical theatre performances, plays, community events, and offering rooms for local groups. It'll be a space for everybody." She inhaled and held up a finger. "And that's not the only thing. Just today, outline planning permission was granted for a dozen new buildings. They will be a mixture of new accommodation and offices. Another jewel in Margate's crown of commerce. We'll soon be as busy as London!"

"That's a surprise," Emily said. "There was some criticism over those plans when they were first submitted. Still, it'll be done tastefully. Everything Lady Lizzie does is tasteful."

"We intend to clear the rot and make Margate even more marvellous than it already is," Lady Lizzie continued.

Although there was more applause, I noted a few people in the crowd grumbling and whispering to each other.

I leaned over to Mabel. "I see there are dissenters."

"Not for the posh arts centre. Everybody wants to see a musical, don't they? But it's the clearing out the rot part we don't all agree with. They're complaining because they're losing their homes." Mabel waved a hand in the air. "Although I don't know why they're moaning. They'll be getting compensation."

Lady Lizzie turned to the side. "Now the formalities are over, it's time to cut the ribbon and announce the new arcade officially open."

A suited man handed her a large pair of scissors, and she made a show of cutting the red ribbon, pausing for several seconds while photographs were taken.

"And now the fun really begins," Mabel said. "Shall we investigate these sparkling new amusements?"

I nodded then dropped back to speak to Matthew. "Are you having fun?"

"It's too noisy. Felix hates it," he muttered.

"You let me know when Felix has had too much, and I'll arrange for you to go back to the hotel."

Matthew shot a desperate look over his shoulder. "I'll stay. Mother will only come back with me, and I don't want to ruin her evening."

"We'll find a quiet spot in the penny arcades. That'll take your mind off things."

He nodded, still clutching Felix's lead and Ruby's arm.

"Shall we try the scenic railway ride?" Ruby asked. "Now I've learned it's less scenic and more pulse-pounding, I'm most interested in having a whizz round."

"You'll be lucky. That's the queue." Mabel pointed out an enormous snaking line that must have been half a mile in length.

"Oh dear. We've left it too late," Ruby said. "We could try later. Perhaps the initial rush will have subsided by then."

"We can buy our tickets now," I said. "Then return and take a ride."

"Count me out," my mother said. "And I've seen Colonel Griffin. He's taking me to look at the community art project, and then we thought we'd try our hand at the penny arcades."

"Be careful in those places," Mabel cautioned. "You'll find pick pocketers lurking."

"I'll join you," Emily said. "Keep an eye on things. And I have an entry in the art project. I wrote a poem and had a local artist illustrate it. I haven't yet seen it on the wall."

My mother and Emily bustled off together and joined Colonel Griffin, who waited patiently for them, wearing a dapper linen suit. He acknowledged my mother with a flourish before cocking out his elbow for her to take. Even if this was a holiday fling, and a so-far platonic one, I was glad to see my mother happy. She'd never get over my father's death—a loss like that left a permanent scar—but we all deserved a second bite of happiness.

A person could be loved and lost, but one's own life shouldn't stop because of their death. We live a full life because they can't. It was a philosophy I stuck to with a rigid intensity.

"Let's explore the new amusements," Ruby said to me. "Jacob, will you join us?"

He turned from examining the crowd. "Of course. I thought I saw someone I recognised."

"I didn't know you had friends in this area," I said.

He shook his head. "It was someone with a passing resemblance to an old colleague, that's all. Where should we go first?"

Ruby led the way through the bustling crowd, and we found ourselves ensconced in a variety of games and quite lost track of time. Two hours passed, and we were all thirsty, with aching feet from so much walking.

I eyed Jacob's leg. His limp had grown more pronounced, so I feigned a yawn. "I need to rest. Join me."

He slid a glance my way then took the seat beside me. "I know what you're doing."

"Resting my feet? This evening has been an adventure. And I didn't realise I was so adept at pin bowling. It was a hoot."

Jacob stretched out his injured leg, stifling a groan. "You don't need to concern yourself with me. I'll let you know when I've had enough."

"You jolly well won't. I know what you're like. You don't want to let anybody down, so you suffer in silence. Have you taken more pain medication?"

"I had a dose just before dinner. You're supposed to take the pills with food."

"Very good. Keep following my orders, and you won't go far wrong."

Jacob relaxed back into the seat and surveyed the crowd. "It was a good choice coming here. Everyone is having so much fun."

"Including you?"

"Surprisingly, yes. And I am truly sorry for being so glum over the last few days. I've got a lot on my mind."

I gently took his hand between both of mine. "I understand. You had a clear path for your future and it's gone. You're rebuilding it one brick at a time. I'd be just like you if our roles were reversed."

"What's your path?"

I squeezed his hand, knowing what was on his mind. "I'm not entirely certain, but I do know there'll always be dogs."

He laughed warmly. "That's a given. But what else? With all this talk about a Kent office, are you considering a permanent relocation?"

"I'm definitely not. But this county is charming, don't you think? I heard someone describe it as the English Tuscany just the other day. They're not wrong."

"I don't know about that, but it is rather lovely," Jacob said.

"Could you imagine living here?" I was treading carefully. After all, relocating to a new part of the country was a huge adventure.

"It's the place I plan to retire to."

Jacob's comment surprised me so much, I lost my words.

He continued, "We sometimes took family holidays here when I was a child. My old dad loved to visit the port in Medway when we were down this way. He was fascinated by the ships coming in and out. There was a big naval presence there as well."

"You could see this as a second home?"

"It was always in my future," Jacob said. "I wouldn't want anywhere big, though. And nothing rural. I like town living. And if my leg never fully heals, long walks will be out of the question."

"I absolutely agree." I drew in a breath. "And you may have noticed, some of the offices we looked at come with accommodation."

"I noticed."

"That would be convenient if staying over."

"It would indeed." Jacob stared at me in silence for several seconds. "While it's just the two of us, there is something I need to talk to you about."

I jerked my hands away and shook my head. "No! Just fun this evening."

"Fun! We were just talking about office space and moving. How is that fun?"

"Starting a new business is exciting," I said. "Is what you want to talk to me about exciting?"

"I wouldn't call it exciting," Jacob said. "But it's important you know about it."

"Then it's not for tonight." My tone brooked no disagreement. Jacob wanted to discuss the status of our relationship, and I hadn't determined what that should be.

"We can't avoid this conversation forever," Jacob said.

"I don't know what you're talking about." I smoothed my hem over my knees.

He fell silent again then sighed. "Are you really sure about starting your own business? You're a forward-thinking woman, but not everyone approves of women being in business. And I know you've had trouble at your uncle's newspaper from the other journalists."

"I can handle a bunch of ill-mannered journalists with outdated ideas," I said. "And times are changing. Women are breaching all barriers. Why shouldn't I set up my own private investigation firm?"

"I don't see how you'll manage," Jacob said. "You work full time at your uncle's newspaper. You have your family to watch over. And you volunteer at the dogs' home."

"That's why I need you as my right-hand man. I'm very capable, but a woman must know her limits." It was time to lay my cards on the table. "I'd like you to lead on setting up the Kent office."

Jacob fell silent again. "I'd be in charge?"

"Nothing's set in stone, so jump to no conclusions, but how would you feel about being the public face of a private investigation service? You have the skills, the knowledge, and the contacts to make this work."

When Jacob didn't immediately reject my idea, hope flooded through me.

"You want me to move to Kent permanently?" he asked.

"It would be easier to run the business if you lived here," I said. "And I'd see plenty of you. I'd visit on weekends, and we could tackle the bigger cases together. You could hire staff. There'd be a budget to do that. You'd make it how you wanted. I wouldn't interfere."

He snorted a laugh.

"Well, I'd interfere as little as possible. What do you say? A fresh start?"

Jacob caught hold of my hand and kissed the back of it. "You're an extraordinary woman, Veronica Vale."

"Thank you." I was so startled by his response that my words came out on a whisper.

"I'm broken, without work, and have been consistently unpleasant to you."

"All true."

"And yet here you are. Do you enjoy being punished?"

"I have heard there are certain women who enjoy mistreatment, but I'm not one of them," I said. "I see through your veneer. You wear this cold indifference, but you have a big heart. You're kind to my family, you sneak Benji treats whenever you think I'm not looking, and you've allowed me to develop my sleuthing skills by working alongside you on taxing cases."

"We never worked alongside each other," he said levelly. "But I acquiesced to your involvement because it was better than being browbeaten."

"I'm no nagging shrew, but I know my own mind, and I speak it well enough." I pressed a finger to his lips as he began to protest. "You're a good man, Jacob. You have the makings of a great man. But you need me by your side. Especially if we go into business together."

"I don't have a lot of money to invest, but I can provide some financial assistance."

I kissed his cheek. "We'll work out all the details later."

He stared at me, his gaze moving to my mouth. "Are we really doing this?"

I gulped. "It would appear so."

"Templeton, is that you?"

Jacob jumped in his seat and turned to look at a thickset man with a short neck and a bulldog-like face striding towards us, a huge smile taking away the stiff edges of sternness and time worn living.

"Bishop? That was you in the crowd! I spotted you earlier. Whatever brings you down here?"

The men firmly shook hands.

"I got a transfer. After all that unpleasant business, I needed a change of scene."

"Oh! Yes. Of course." Jacob turned to me. "Veronica, may I introduce you to my old colleague, Geoffrey Bishop."

I stood and shook Geoffrey's hand. "It's a pleasure to meet you, Mr Bishop."

"Please, call me Bishop. Everyone does. Mr Bishop was my father, and Geoffrey is so stuffy. I'm sorry for interrupting, but when I saw Templeton here, I had to say hello. This is a turn-up for the books." His gaze went to Jacob's leg. "Got an injury?"

"It's a long story."

"I'll take you for a pint of ale, and we can discuss it." Bishop glanced at me. "Unless you have another engagement."

"You gentlemen catch up," I said. "I intend to find the others and then return to the hotel. See you tomorrow?"

For a second, Jacob looked torn, then he nodded. "Until tomorrow." He walked off with his friend, their heads together, deep in conversation.

I clasped my hands against my chest. This evening couldn't have worked out any more splendidly. Jacob was open to the possibility of running the private investigation firm in Kent, and he had a friend here to chum around with. Everything was fitting into place.

It took me a good half an hour to track down my mother and Colonel Griffin. Emily had disappeared.

"There you are," I said.

My mother held up a paper cup full of pennies. "I won! The first time I put in a coin. Colonel Griffin is my good luck charm."

"You have all the luck you need, my dear lady," he said.

"Where's Emily?" I asked.

"I think she got bored from being stuck with two oldies," my mother said. "She headed off to speak to Lady Lizzie."

"And Ruby?" I asked.

"I saw her talking to those French chaps." My mother was feeding coins into a machine.

"You mean the Italians?"

"Yes. Something like that. Dark hair and lovely accents. Tall, too."

"Where did they go?" I persisted.

"I didn't think to ask. Look, I got two in a row. Does that mean anything?"

"I'm afraid not, my dear," Colonel Griffin said. "Try again."

"What about Matthew?" I asked.

"He decided he'd had enough of the noise. He took Felix back to the hotel."

"You let him go on his own?"

"He was fine," my mother said.

"He looked tired," Colonel Griffin said. "But I watched him walk along the promenade with his dog. They were perfectly safe."

"Thank you. I appreciate you doing that," I said. I'd have to chastise my mother in the morning for neglecting Matthew. This adventure was the first he'd taken in a long time, and I didn't want it to overwhelm him because he'd never do it again.

I passed the time browsing the amusements while my mother spent down her pennies. Within an hour, she'd lost her winnings and decided she no longer liked the penny slots, so after saying goodnight to Colonel Griffin, we walked back to the hotel, arm in arm, while I listened to my mother tell me all about the wonderful evening she'd had with Colonel Griffin and what a gentleman he was.

After settling Benji and giving him his supper, I washed my face and got into my nightgown, making myself a small cup of tea before sitting up to wait for Ruby to return. She also needed speaking to about gallivanting off with two strangers, no matter how handsome they were.

My head jerked up when someone knocked on my door. The tea had grown cold beside me, so I must have been asleep for at least half an hour.

"Ruby, have you forgotten your key?" I hurried to the door and pulled it open. It wasn't Ruby standing outside, but Mabel, and she was in tears.

"Whatever's the matter?" I asked.

She choked back a sob. "It's Emily. She's drowned."

Chapter 4

The wind blasted off the sea, feeling like it was cutting through to the bone as we stood huddled close to the pier, struggling to see what was going on. After Mabel had shown up at my hotel room door so distressed, I'd gathered Jacob and Benji, and we'd dashed with her to the pier to learn more.

"Veronica! What the devil is going on?" Ruby appeared, one of her handsome new Italian companions beside her.

"There's been an accident," I said. "Emily's drowned."

"No! Surely not." Ruby squinted at the pier. "Did she fall?"

"The police think it was an accident." Mabel hugged herself, her teeth chattering more from shock than the cold.

I wrapped a comforting arm around her. Emily had the whole world at her feet. It seemed cruel that her opportunities had vanished in the blink of an eye because of a tragic error.

"Aren't there barriers to stop people from falling off the pier?" Ruby asked.

"Of course there are! None of this makes sense," Mabel said.

"Could Emily have gone swimming?" Jacob asked. "She might have got turned around in the darkness and headed in the wrong direction or been caught in a current and grown too tired to keep fighting to get back to the shore."

"Emily would never swim at night. She was raised by the sea, so she knows its dangers. She could always identify a riptide. Besides, she wasn't much of a swimmer. More of a paddler." Mabel sniffed back more tears. "Why aren't the police telling me anything? They must know what happened by now."

"I'll see if I can find out what's going on. Bishop is most likely involved." Jacob gently squeezed my elbow before limping away.

"Does your fella have connections?" Mabel asked.

"Until recently, he was employed as a police inspector in London," I said. "You may have noticed his limp, which means he's no longer fit for duty, so he's exploring other options."

"He's a handy one to have around if he can help," Mabel said.

We stood in a tense silence for several minutes, the sharp sea breeze whipping up worrying thoughts of what happened to Emily.

"Are you going to introduce me to your new friend?" I asked Ruby, casting a pointed look at the silent, handsome man beside her.

"Oh! In the shock, I forgot you haven't been introduced." Ruby turned to her friend. "You go home,

Alfonso. I'll find you tomorrow, and you can get to know Veronica in happier circumstances."

"Are you sure, charming lady? I don't want to leave you while you're distressed." His speech pattern was a rapid Italian staccato with a warm depth to it.

"I'm quite well. And I'm with friends. We look after each other." Ruby stood on her tiptoes and kissed his cheek. "Ciao."

"Ciao, bella." He nodded with a smile then slid off into the darkness.

"The police are moving something." Mabel pressed a hand to her mouth before lowering it. "It could be Emily."

"How did you find out what happened?" Ruby asked.

"I know the local beat copper, Jimmy Cross. As soon as he heard Emily's name, he knocked on the pub door. I dashed straight to Veronica for help."

"We're here for whatever you need. And we'll get to the bottom of things." I kept my arm around Mabel's shoulders as a source of comfort, hoping it would help a touch.

There was nothing we could do but wait and watch. The police took another ten minutes, but finally a covered body, which could only be Emily, was brought onto the main road and settled in the back of a black police van.

"Do you know who found Emily?" I asked as softly as I could.

"A couple who'd had too much to drink, looking for a quiet spot on the beach," Mabel said. "The police have already spoken to them. They're not local, just down for a few days' holiday. They were walking along the sand,

and they saw what they thought was a lump of wood. It was only when they got closer that they realised it was my Emily." She started crying again.

"It's so sad," Ruby said. "Where did Emily go after we all met at the amusements?"

Mabel sniffed back tears. "She mentioned taking a walk. I was busy with all the entertainments going on, and I didn't have a second to myself when I returned to the pub. The last time I saw her, she was headed off in the crowd."

"Emily was well-known and liked around here," I said. "People would have seen her. We'll figure out her movements and learn what she was doing on the pier so late."

"Goodness. It is later than I realised." Ruby shook her wrist as if not believing the time displayed. "I made a promise to myself to be back at the hotel by midnight."

It was two hours past that time.

"You had an extremely attractive distraction," I murmured.

Ruby's blush was even detectable in the gloom. "Alfonso is splendid. And such a smooth talker. That accent makes me weak at the knees."

"Not too weak, I hope. You've only just met the fellow."

Jacob returned from his mission. "I found Bishop. I grabbed a few words, but he's busy."

"What did he tell you?" I asked.

"At the moment, the police are unsure what happened," Jacob said. "They received a panicked telephone call from a couple who found Emily on the beach."

"She definitely drowned?" I asked.

Jacob nodded. "It seems most likely. Of course, they need to do a thorough investigation to be certain. And in this poor light, it's difficult to find useful evidence. There's talk of a fall if she'd been drinking or a possible swimming accident."

"Emily wasn't much of a swimmer, and never at night," Mabel said. "She enjoyed a drink now and again, but she wouldn't get so drunk as to stumble into the waves."

"There's little we can do at the moment," I said. "We should all go home and regroup in the morning."

"I won't be able to get a wink of sleep," Mabel said.

"We'll come back with you and stay at the Harbour Arms for the night," I said. "I don't want you on your own."

Mabel's tense expression relaxed. "I have guests in some of the rooms, but I can squeeze you in. It would be nice to have company."

"Then it's settled. Ruby and I will return with Mabel to the Harbour Arms. Benji too. Jacob, you go back to the hotel. Mother and Matthew will need to be told what's going on first thing. And then I'd appreciate it if you could go to the police station to see if there are any updates. Come straight to the pub as soon as you have helpful news."

He nodded, not minding one bit that I was barking orders. The poor chap was used to it.

"I don't want to put you to any bother," Mabel said.

"Helping a friend in need is no bother at all," I said. "Let's go to the pub. You're freezing, and you need a restorative brandy before bed."

"So do I," Ruby said. "What a dreadful shock."

After a brief farewell to Jacob, I escorted a shivering Mabel on the short walk back to the Harbour Arms. She took little persuading to have a large brandy, and we sat for an hour talking about Emily and attempting to figure out how she ended up on the beach. None of us came to any suitable conclusion. So, with heavy hearts and tired eyes, we retired to our beds. In the morning, the investigation would begin.

I didn't think I'd be able to sleep, but Mabel's beds were delightfully comfortable, and I woke refreshed and ready to face the day. A wave of sadness washed over me as I recalled the events of the previous evening. But tears wouldn't help Emily.

After a quick wash and tidy up in the nearby bathroom, I left my room with Benji beside me and tapped on Ruby's door. She was already up and about, so we headed down the stairs, following the delicious scents of cooking breakfast from the kitchen.

Mabel stood by the table, holding a frying pan, just dishing up some delicious sausages. "Good morning, ladies. I hope you're hungry."

"You should have let us do that," Ruby said.

"I prefer to keep busy." Mabel tossed a piece of sausage to Benji. "We can eat in here. The dining room is set for guests, and they don't want to be overhearing our conversation now, do they?"

"Are you sure we can't lend a hand?" I asked. "Although I should warn you, Ruby is a terror in the kitchen, and I'm not much better. I rely heavily on

Matthew's excellent cooking. He served a stint in the army and picked up useful skills."

"That's good of you to offer, but I don't want my kitchen catching fire and having something else to deal with. Besides, it's almost done. I'm just waiting for the toast."

I was happy to be relieved from a potentially unsuccessful attempt at making breakfast. Once we were settled in our seats, each with a large plate of cooked breakfast and big cups of strong brown tea, Mabel let out a sigh.

"I've been thinking about Emily most of the night."

"Did you get any sleep?" Ruby paused from cutting into a sausage.

"Here and there," Mabel said.

"I can help at the pub today," I said. "Give you a rest. I've pulled my fair share of pints over the years, and I can handle the customers."

"I've got my team here, and as I said, keeping busy is better than sitting in a chair and staring into space. It helps nobody. And Emily wouldn't want that. She was so full of life, and I intend to go on living even though she's not."

"Well said," I agreed. "But if there's anything you need, we're here. And we can extend our stay. Jacob has no work to return to, and Uncle Harry is always obliging when it comes to my job at the newspaper."

"Don't mess up your life because I'm in a pickle." Mabel leaned over and patted my hand. "Of course, you're always welcome. You're such a good girl. Your father brought you up well. So did your mother."

"They did their best," I said. "I like to think I make them proud."

"No doubt about that. Eat up. You don't want the food getting cold."

Twenty minutes later, plates were clear, and we were politely refusing more toast.

"If you feed me anything else, I'll have to undo a top button," Ruby said. "I haven't had such a delicious breakfast in years. I usually stick to small portions."

I stifled a laugh. Never a falser word had been spoken, especially when there was a dessert trolley in sight.

"It was my pleasure." Mabel cleared the plates and refilled our cups with more strong tea. A knock at the back door sent her hurrying over, and she opened it to reveal Jacob outside. She ushered him in and pressed upon him tea and a bacon sandwich before he even had a chance to sit down.

He mumbled his thanks. "I was up early and went to the police station. I wanted to see if there was an update on Emily."

I nodded for him to continue.

"It was busy. It took me time to track down Bishop."

"I've been thinking about what could have happened all night," Mabel said. "I know my girl, and she's smart. She wouldn't stumble off a pier or decide it was a good idea to go for a midnight swim. She was bright and sensible. That young lady was going places, and I was happy to support her when she did."

I set down my cup, my stomach unsettled. "Mabel, if you don't believe this was an accident, do you think it was deliberate?"

Mabel drew in a shaky breath. "I reckon so."

"What makes you so sure someone else was involved in Emily's death?" Jacob sat upright and alert, like an eager cocker spaniel about to launch after a ball.

Mabel looked around the table before taking a sip from her cup, her hand shaking only a fraction as she settled it back down. "Emily told me she'd been chased."

"When was this?" I asked.

"A few weeks ago," Mabel said. "Emily was coming back from researching a story, and it was late. She said she got the sense she was being watched, and when she looked over her shoulder, a man was following her."

"Did she get a good look at this man?" I asked.

"No. It was late evening, and not all the streets around here have lighting. She was always one to follow her instincts, though. She told me it's how she got the inside scoop on all the juicy stories. Rather than continuing to walk to the pub, Emily changed her route to see if the man would follow."

"I take it he did?" Jacob asked.

Mabel nodded. "She made three left turns, which took her back to her original route, and he did exactly the same. That's when Emily ran for her life."

"And he chased after her?" I asked.

"He did. But she was light on her feet and speedy, so she got away. She dashed into a late-night café and waited for a group to leave before heading out with them. She checked around carefully, but whoever was chasing her had gone. Emily came straight back here and told me all about it."

"Did Emily report this matter to the police?" Jacob asked.

"No, she was rattled, but she said there was no point in telling the police because they wouldn't be able to do anything. She couldn't identify the man because it was so dark."

"Gosh," Ruby said. "Do you think this man followed Emily to the beach and confronted her about something?"

"It's possible," Mabel said. "Just like Veronica, Emily was fearless and extremely nosy."

"That's an accurate description," Jacob said.

I gently kicked him under the table, avoiding his bad leg. "Was Emily working on any scandalous stories? Something that could have got her into trouble?"

"She was always working on a big story," Mabel said. "She had several she was researching."

"Emily mentioned to me last night that she wanted to talk about them. It was so hectic in the amusements that we didn't get a moment to ourselves, but I promised we'd catch up soon. Perhaps she was going to tell me about being followed or feeling threatened," I said.

"Even if she had, there would be little you could have done," Ruby said. "And you couldn't have predicted her death."

I nodded, but it was still a blow that I hadn't given the young journalist more attention. "Did Emily keep notes about her articles? They could help us figure out what happened."

"Copious amounts of notes. She was always scribbling in one notepad or another. I can go through her things and look for information that could help. Emily kept everything in her bedroom. She had a little office set up where she worked when she wasn't at the library, archive, or interviewing people." Mabel dabbed away a tear. "This place will seem quiet without her. She brimmed with ideas and life."

"She got that from you," I said. "You looked after her so well."

"I had no children, so it was a delight to open my doors to her. Emily was like a daughter to me," Mabel said.

We allowed Mabel a moment with her grief, sipping our tea as Benji gently rested his head in Mabel's lap to comfort her.

"I'd like to look at those notebooks," Jacob said. "And I believe the police will be interested in them, too."

"I should hope they would be," I said. "When they learn Emily was chased, they'll be keen on hunting down that man and hearing what he's about."

"I'm sure they will." Jacob drew in a breath, his expression stern. "And although it's early days in the investigation, unfortunately, Mabel could be right. The police now believe Emily was murdered."

Chapter 5

I pushed back my seat, my spine tense. "What evidence is there of murder?"

Jacob turned to Mabel. "I don't want to upset you."

"I insist on hearing everything." Mabel pressed her hands flat on the table.

I nodded at Jacob. Mabel was made of stern stuff.

"The police can't be certain, so don't jump to conclusions, but there were marks on Emily's body that are suspicious." Jacob cast me a warning look. He knew how quick I was to spring into action without having a full account of the facts. "I could only speak to Bishop for a moment before he was called away. Apparently, murders around here are few and far between, so this has caused a stir at the station."

Mabel sucked in a deep, shaky breath. "That's true. It's one of the reasons I love living here. What can you tell us about these marks?"

I gestured for Jacob to continue, even though he looked hesitant.

"There were marks on Emily's arms and legs. It suggests a struggle before she died."

Mabel thumped a fist on the table. "Good! I hope she grievously injured whoever did this to her, and they're sorry they ever met her."

"Emily was no shrinking violet," I said. "If the man who chased her discovered her on the pier, or she fled there and got trapped, she wouldn't have gone quietly. I'm sure they're nursing a number of bruises."

"That gives me a small degree of satisfaction," Mabel said.

"Could it have been a fight with a chap she was fond of?" Ruby asked. "Was Emily involved with a gentleman?"

Mabel shook her head. "There was no one special in her life. Her work kept her too busy for flirting and flipping her lashes at a passing fancy."

"Trouble with any other family members?" Jacob asked.

"No family troubles. I'm her only living family," Mabel said. "Everybody else is dead, thanks to the war or ill-health. Her parents have been gone for years. No siblings, either."

"What was your relationship with Emily like?" Jacob slipped into police interview mode, which deserved him another kick for being so tactless.

"Emily was a headstrong young girl, who occasionally needed reminding not to get too full of herself, but we bumped along nicely together. She even helped behind the bar when someone was off sick. She was kind like that."

"What were you doing around midnight last night?" Jacob asked.

"Now is not the time for that question," I said sharply. "Mabel had nothing to do with this."

"Why would I want Emily dead?" Mabel's tone was spiked with anger, her eyes bright with tears. "We adored each other."

"I've known Mabel and Emily for a long time," I said. "I'll vouch for their relationship. And my father always had good things to say about Mabel."

"He could always rely on me, God rest his soul," Mabel said. "I was worried about what would happen to the Harbour Arms when he died, but I was glad you took over the business affairs. Everything's been ticking along nicely."

"I never had any doubts about your ability to do a splendid job," I said. "And I know Emily admired your hard work and dedication."

Mabel sniffed. "She did, but she said I should have loftier goals than running a pub. I told her I was a career woman. I have my own business, and the pub turns over a healthy profit. The trouble was, Emily had bigger ambitions. And look where they got her."

"Do you really think a story she was investigating led to her death?" Ruby asked.

"It makes sense to me," Mabel said. "She always said if you scratched the surface of any seemingly idyllic place, you uncovered the truth, and that truth was often unpleasant. She must have discovered something that put a target on her back. Silly girl. She would have been safer working in the pub and pulling pints with me."

"You still haven't told me your alibi," Jacob said.

Mabel narrowed her eyes at him. "I spent most of the evening with all of you. When it got late, I came back to the pub to see how everything was going. It had been a busy night, and we had plenty of punters in. I stayed behind with Cathy to tidy and sent her home around midnight. I did a bit more cleaning and then headed up to bed."

"What time did the police alert you about what had happened to Emily?" I asked.

"Jimmy showed up, kicking the door and hollering around one-thirty," Mabel said. "Gave me a fright. I thought someone was trying to break in. I have a room at the front, so I pulled up the sash window and yelled at him. I could tell by the look on his face there was a problem, so I rushed down, and that's when I learned about Emily. I ran straight to the Harbour Arms to find you."

"Not that we need your alibi, but it's clear you had nothing to do with this." I shot a stern look at Jacob.

He grumbled to himself. "I need to cover all the bases. The police will ask the same question."

They would. So it was good Mabel was prepared. "Mabel, I know this is a terrible shock, but if you can think of anybody Emily had a run-in with, it could be the clue we need to figure out what happened to her."

Mabel pressed her lips together. "Not so long ago, she had heated words with our local doctor. When I asked about it, she said they were discussing an article she wanted to write, but she didn't have enough evidence to publish."

"Evidence about what?" I asked.

"Emily wouldn't say. She said I could read about it when she got a front-page feature. Of course, I teased her about that. But perhaps I shouldn't have. She was determined to make herself a success."

"Remind me of your doctor's name?" I asked.

"Doctor Richard Patterson," Mabel said. "He's not behind this, though. He's got a kind nature, and when he's not working, he looks after his sick wife. She's been unwell for years, and he's so patient with her. He has her at home and does everything for her. He's a good man."

"There's no harm in starting there," I said. "We can go now."

"Should we interfere?" Jacob asked. "Bishop is a capable chap. If there was foul play, he'll get to the bottom of it. He's solved almost as many murders as me."

I resisted the desire to tell him many of those solutions had been thanks to my involvement. "There's no harm in finding useful information and passing it on to the police. Besides, Mabel is a friend, and I respected Emily. We must ensure justice is done."

Jacob opened his mouth as if to state a protest then nodded.

"Do you need me for this?" asked Ruby.

I turned to her. "Have you got other plans for today?"

"Now you have Jacob and Benji to help, I promised I'd spend the day with Alfonso."

"Goodness me. You spent last night with him. Surely, you must be bored with each other by now."

Ruby blushed. "I can't get enough of his accent. Of course, I could cancel…"

I glanced at Jacob. "I have a worthy stand-in. But let's not make this a habit. Jacob doesn't have your unique talents."

"I know how to run an investigation," Jacob said. "And I've got much more experience than either of you."

"We have a much higher success rate than you," I said. "And no one can bat an eyelash quite like Ruby."

He grumbled under his breath. "I concede that point. But don't forget we have an office to view at noon. Or do you want to cancel?"

"There's no need to cancel or delay progress. We'll go immediately to Doctor Patterson and find out what words were exchanged with Emily."

After getting Doctor Patterson's address from Mabel and promising to give her an update as soon as we had anything useful, I headed outside with Jacob and Benji. Ruby dashed off in the other direction, already dressed up for a day with her new Italian friend. When I had a moment to consider this relationship, I'd speak to her. I didn't want a holiday romance spilling over into anything more serious. If Alfonso was a performer, that meant he travelled extensively, so they'd never see each other. And Ruby adored attention. She also deserved it.

"How is Mabel doing?" Jacob asked me.

"She was handling herself well until you blundered in and practically accused her of killing Emily," I said, a touch of sour tart in my tone.

"I barely did that," Jacob said. He sighed. "But I am sorry if I offended her. It's a force of habit."

"You do often say things that I find offensive."

"Veronica! I didn't mean that. I meant questioning suspects."

"I know. I'm teasing."

"What I said is true. It is often a family member who's involved."

I put my hand through his crooked elbow. "No harm done. You were just a little tactless. But I'll vouch for Mabel. And if you must, you can always speak to her barmaid Cathy to make sure they were together. But I'd bet the house on it not being her."

"Then we need to focus on the doctor," Jacob said.

"And anyone else Emily recently argued with," I added. "Emily was clever. If she got the sniff of a scandal, she'd relentlessly chase it."

"I know someone else like that," Jacob said. "And I also know the kind of trouble she finds herself in."

"You'll have to introduce me to this woman sometime. She sounds a marvellous hoot. We could swap stories."

Jacob shook his head, though there was a smile on his face.

"You love doing this, don't you?" I asked.

"Walking with you and Benji along the seafront?"

"No! Although that is pleasant. I mean solving crimes. It's in your blood. You need to run the private investigation office. It's exactly the cure for your ills."

Jacob walked in silence for a long moment. "I believe you're right. A change of scene and a new occupation would be just the ticket. Provided you're involved."

"As if I'd leave you to run things. You'd only make a mess."

He chuckled. "We can't have that. Very well. We'll see how this office viewing goes at lunchtime and take it from there."

If the current situation hadn't been so serious, I'd have done a little skip of delight.

We arrived at a quaint cottage with faded roses around the door and a neat garden full of salt-tolerant plants at the front. We received no answer when we knocked, so we walked around to the back of the house and discovered Doctor Patterson in a chair next to a lady wearing a large sun hat with a blanket draped over her knees. I had to assume that was his wife.

"Hello there. I don't mean to startle you, but we knocked on the front door and didn't get an answer," I said.

Doctor Patterson turned in his seat. "I recognise you from last night. Your mother asked about her sore feet. Is she still suffering?"

"My mother's feet are excellent." I made the introductions. "But I'm sorry to bring bad news. Emily Brewer was found dead on the beach last night."

"Oh! Yes, of course. I heard, although I wasn't there last night. I'm unable to leave my wife for long periods of time. This is Patricia." Doctor Patterson stood and gestured to his wife.

The lady in the large sun hat barely moved, other than a faint dip of the chin.

"Where are my manners? Please, have a seat. Would you like something to drink?" Doctor Patterson fussed around us until we were settled in seats.

"We're fine, thank you," I said. "I'm friends with Mabel from the Harbour Arms. I'm also her employer."

"Of course! Of course!" Doctor Patterson returned to his seat. "I knew that wasn't the first time I'd seen you. You sometimes visit the pub, don't you?"

"I do. Although I've recently been remiss. I live in London, so it's not always easy to get down." I glanced at Doctor Patterson's wife, but she sat still and silent. "I have some questions about Emily. We're trying to figure out what happened to her. I always considered her a bright young thing, so I'm shocked by the situation."

"You must be."

"And... I'm looking for answers."

Doctor Patterson paused. "I'm not sure what help I can be to you. Emily wasn't one of my patients. In fact, I've recently reduced my hours to focus on my wife." He gently adjusted the blanket over her knees. "I'm even considering retiring from practice."

"Are you not well, Mrs Patterson?" I asked her.

She mumbled something that I didn't catch.

"My wife is very sick," Doctor Patterson said. "I want to spend as much time with her as possible."

"That's decent of you." I glanced at Jacob, and he nodded at me to keep pushing. "Could you tell me about the argument you had with Emily recently?"

Doctor Patterson jerked back in his seat, a nervy hand smoothing his mustache. "We didn't argue. We didn't know each other well enough to argue. What makes you ask that question?"

"Oh. Perhaps I'm mistaken," I said. "Mabel was certain you'd had harsh words. She saw you together recently, and things appeared heated. Emily wouldn't tell her what was going on, but she was concerned."

Doctor Patterson scrubbed his chin and stared off into the distance. He clicked his fingers together. "I know what that was. A silly accident and all my fault. I trod on Emily's foot and didn't realise it. She took offence and demanded an apology."

"That was it?" I asked.

"What else could it be? Are you sure I can't get either of you a drink?" Doctor Patterson gestured to the house. "I always keep something cool on tap for my wife."

"No, thank you," Jacob said. "Was that the only time you had a falling out with Emily?"

"My social circle has severely diminished as my wife's health has declined," Doctor Patterson said with a sad smile. "When I'm not working, I take care of her needs. I can't remember the last time I went to a social event. And certainly not with a younger crowd."

"You were at the opening of the new amusements last night," I said.

"For a few moments. And I have a neighbour who looks in on Patricia when I'm not about. We can't risk you getting into any trouble now, can we, my dear?" Doctor Patterson touched his wife's knee.

I peered closely at Patricia. From outward appearances, she seemed healthy, but she was barely stirring in her seat. She wasn't elderly, so I couldn't figure out what was wrong with her.

"What did you think of Emily's career choice?" I asked.

"She worked at the Harbour Arms, didn't she?" Doctor Patterson said.

"Emily was a journalist," I said. "She received training thanks to a scholarship from Lady Lizzie."

"Oh! I remember something about that. I barely have time to read the newspapers these days. Did she work on the local newspaper?"

"Not yet," I said, "but she was talented and hard-working. She was always chasing a story. I wondered if perhaps she spoke to you because she wanted to publish something about you. Perhaps something from your past."

"Sadly, my past is as dull as my present." Doctor Patterson glanced at his wife before leaning closer to us. "I've dedicated my life to the service of others. I always wanted to be a doctor, although I never thought I'd need to direct my talents towards my own dear wife. I'm considering going into private practice in the future. After..." Although he didn't say it, it was easy to assume he meant after Patricia died. How tragic. What she had must be terminal.

"You never treated Emily for any illnesses or health concerns?" Jacob asked.

"No, and I'm not sure where she was registered," Doctor Patterson said. "Perhaps she wasn't. Whenever I saw her, she was bounding around, looking as healthy as a horse. I'm really sorry, there is little I can tell you about her."

"Did you ever see her having problems with anyone else?" I asked. "She was recently chased home, which rather scared her."

"Chased! How terrifying. It's the first I've heard about that," Doctor Patterson said. "We weren't friends. I knew Emily on sight, of course, because I sometimes drink at the Harbour Arms, but I never saw her having troubles. Perhaps an overly enthusiastic boyfriend?"

"We're pursuing all possibilities," Jacob said.

"Are you with the local police?" Doctor Patterson asked. "Just joined?"

"I'm... an inspector," Jacob replied smoothly, declining to mention he was now a former inspector.

"You must be new to the force. What a case to begin with. Well, welcome aboard." Doctor Patterson shook Jacob's hand before looking at me. "Please, pass on my condolences to Mabel."

"We will," I said.

"If you'll excuse me, I'm exhausted. I was up most of the night with Patricia." Doctor Patterson stood from his seat.

"You were here all night?" I asked.

"Yes, I had a brief stop at the amusements to show my face and then came home. Patricia had a difficult evening. Sometimes, she has night terrors and is unable to settle. I sat up with her and read while she dozed. It's now time for her nap. I may join her."

"Of course. Thank you for your time." We also stood, and after a brief goodbye, headed out of the garden.

I glanced over my shoulder to see Doctor Patterson assisting his wife through the back door into the house. She really was struggling. Perhaps she had a muscle wasting disease. How terrible for someone not yet in middle age.

I nudged Jacob. "What did you think of him?"

"I'm not sure I trust him," Jacob said. "You?"

"I think our good doctor is lying about something."

Chapter 6

"The rooms seemed dark," I said. "You'll need plenty of natural light while you work."

"They seemed fine to me." Jacob strolled along beside me and Benji as we took some sea air after viewing a potential new office. "It's a good location. Close to the train station to make your visits easier."

"I must make sure you're comfortable." I dodged two children so engrossed in eating their sticks of rock, they almost bumped into me.

"I could be comfortable there," Jacob said.

"What about the upstairs accommodation? It was basic."

"But clean and tidy. You could add feminine touches if you'd like."

"You may have better feminine touches than I do," I said tartly. "Besides, I don't know your tastes."

"They're simple. You need to stop fussing. You're not my mother."

"Heavens forbid."

He grinned. "That would be unfortunate. There's Bishop!" Jacob hailed his friend, and after checking the traffic, we crossed the road to a small seaside café where we'd arranged to meet Bishop after viewing the office.

"How did it go?" Bishop asked as he greeted us both.

"I'm not convinced it's the right one for us," I said. "We'll keep looking."

"The space works for me," Jacob said. "But Veronica is the boss."

"And don't you forget it," I said. "Shall we eat? I'm famished."

"It's why I suggested we meet here." Bishop led us inside the small blue-and-white café with a jaunty seaside theme. "They do the best cockles and whelks you've ever tasted."

"Any jellied eels?" Jacob settled into his seat.

"If that's your fancy." Bishop wrinkled his nose.

"I may have a fishcake," I said. "I don't like my seafood chewy. Have you seen Ruby? She said she'd meet us here after we made the arrangements this morning."

"Not yet," Bishop said.

I sighed. "She's often running late. You get used to it."

"Do you want to wait for her?" Bishop was eyeing the chalkboard menu with an eagerness that suggested he was only being polite by asking that question.

"No. It's her own fault if she misses the food."

The waitress came over and took our order, and I added a small cup of cockles for Benji, who unfortunately had to remain outside, tied to a lamppost in full view, and content to watch the passing walkers as he wagged his tail. Once the waitress left, we got down to business.

"You mentioned on the telephone you were suspicious of Doctor Patterson." Bishop appeared cautious. "I like the man. He's a loner, but people talk highly of him."

"He seemed on edge when we spoke to him about Emily," I said.

"We took him by surprise by showing up unannounced, but he wasn't comfortable with our questioning," Jacob said. "And he was focused on his wife. Do you know what's wrong with her?"

"No, and I don't like to ask. But I believe she's been unwell for years," Bishop said. "I wouldn't waste your time on the doctor. We need to look elsewhere."

"Is there any new information on the case?" Jacob asked. "A lead?"

"We've been making enquiries, but so far, no eyewitnesses have come forward," Bishop said. "But our body man is convinced it was murder. There are defensive marks on Emily's arms."

"Those marks couldn't have happened when she was in the water?" Jacob asked. "Perhaps she ended up under the pier and the waves tossed her around."

"It seems unlikely," Bishop said. "The tide was going out, so it would have dragged her towards the horizon."

I shook my head at the grisly conversation. "Poor Mabel. It's so wrong Emily was murdered."

"I agree with you. I knew Emily. She was bright and determined," Bishop said. "But she stood on plenty of toes. She wasn't popular with everybody."

"Who didn't like her?" I asked.

"We're going over the old files to see if anything stands out," Bishop said. "There were several complaints about her trespassing on private property."

"In pursuit of a story, no doubt," I said.

"Most likely. Emily had big ambitions," Bishop said. "She'd often stop by the police station to get information about cases we were working on. Of course, I could give her few details, but she never gave up. And I read some of her writing. She was excellent at what she did."

There was a pause in the conversation as our food was served. The door to the café was pushed open as Ruby dashed in, looking windswept and happy. She was carrying a newspaper-wrapped bundle of chips in one hand. As she took a step inside the café, an enormous seagull swooped down and ripped the chips out of her hand. Ruby screamed and staggered back, causing everyone to look.

Benji barked fiercely at the misbehaving seagull as it swooped away with a beak full of Ruby's chips, scattering the rest on the ground.

Bishop dashed over, catching hold of Ruby's elbow to make sure she was unharmed. "Those seagulls are such beggars! I've seen them grab ice creams from children's hands."

"Ruby always knows how to make an entrance," Jacob murmured.

"Did you see that?" Ruby arrived at the table, ably guided by Bishop. "An enormous bird almost pecked my eyes out."

"It was after your chips," I said.

"If it weren't for Benji and Bishop's bravery, I would have been in trouble." Ruby brushed down her dress then looked back mournfully at her chips. "They were delicious. I'd only had a few."

"You can reward Benji with these." I gave her a small cup of cockles. "Then join us. I'll share my fishcake and chips with you."

After Ruby delivered Benji's delicious treat for being such a hero, she returned to the table. "Sorry I'm late. Alfonso is most distracting."

"I'm glad you could tear yourself away," I said. "We were getting an update about the investigation from Bishop. He was about to tell us who had made formal complaints about Emily."

"Hold on a minute. This is an active investigation," Bishop said. "I can't hand out facts willy-nilly, or I'll find myself in trouble with the chief."

"I can vouch for Veronica and Ruby," Jacob said. "They've assisted me in a number of cases. So has Benji."

Bishop's eyebrows lifted. "They worked for the police in London?"

"In an unofficial capacity," Jacob said. "Veronica enjoys solving puzzles."

"And I have a knack for it," I said. "We'll be discreet, but we must get to the bottom of what happened to Emily. I assure you, if you share information with us, it goes no further. We're not nosy, but we need all the facts if we're to solve this terrible business."

A smile played on Bishop's lips as he glanced at Jacob. "We've known each other long enough to respect each other's opinion. If Templeton says you're good, then you're good with me, too."

"So you'll reveal who put in a complaint about Emily trespassing on their property?" I asked.

Bishop forked several whelks and popped them into his mouth. "Emily was looking into a story on Tommy

McAllister. She jumped over a fence at the back of one of his clubs. It's a place I don't recommend going on your holiday. You get a rowdy type drinking there."

"What was Emily looking for?" I asked.

"I never could get to the bottom of that," Bishop said. "But Tommy is no fool and protects his assets. He has dogs guarding his properties and sometimes patrol guards. The dogs started barking when Emily poked around. That alerted the patrolman, and he chased her off."

"Did Tommy bring charges against Emily for trespassing?" I asked.

"No, but he was quick enough to tell me to warn her off, saying she'd find herself in trouble if she poked into business that had nothing to do with her," Bishop said.

"That's our man!" Ruby said. "These chips are delicious. I wish I had my own."

"I'll get you a plate." Bishop hopped up and headed to the counter.

"You need to be careful not to steal his heart as well as your new Italian friend's," I teased.

"Be careful with Bishop," Jacob said quietly.

"Is he not to be trusted?" I asked.

"It's nothing to do with that. We've been friends for a long time, and he's of good character." Jacob made sure Bishop wasn't listening before leaning closer. "He's a widower. His wife died during one of the London bombings, and he's never fully recovered. He was quick to request a transfer down to Kent when the chance arose."

"He needed a fresh start," I said. "I don't blame him after such a tragedy."

"Fear not, Jacob," Ruby said. "I'm sure your friend is a darling, but I'm occupied with Alfonso."

"Don't get in over your head with this Italian Lothario," I said.

"I'm very much in charge of the situation," Ruby said. "And if things keep going so well, you'll have to meet formally. And if you're interested, his friend is also single."

I glanced at Jacob. "My attentions lie elsewhere."

Ruby grinned as she stole another chip from my plate. "I'm happy to hear that."

Bishop returned with Ruby's chips, and we spent a moment enjoying the delicious food. Somehow, being in the sea air made everything tastier, and my appetite thrived.

"What can you tell us about Tommy?" I asked Bishop.

Bishop set down his fork, his expression serious. "The best word to describe him is shady. I wouldn't trust him as far as I could throw him."

"Are his businesses not legitimate?" Jacob asked.

"On the surface, there's a veneer of respectability, but there's something dodgy about the way he runs things." Bishop looked out the window. "And the man makes far too much money. It can't all come from his amusements and the clubs."

"How many clubs does he own?" I asked.

"Two. And the older part of the amusements. The more rundown area with the penny arcades."

"I was there last night with my mother," I said. "They were good fun. Although she lost all of her winnings."

"Perhaps that's how Tommy makes his money," Ruby said. "He fixes the machines, so nobody ever wins."

"We're talking serious amounts of cash," Bishop said. "But Tommy keeps his books up to date and has never been caught doing anything illegal. Some people see him as a local man come good. He had a rough start, but he was determined to pull himself out of the gutter and make something of himself. His old man was a criminal, though. Died in prison."

"Perhaps Tommy is respectable, but is unable to shake off the shackles of his past," I said.

"I can't put my finger on it, but there's a whiff of scandal about him," Bishop said. "I always trust my gut, and it's telling me Tommy isn't to be trusted. He's dangerous. I wouldn't want to be on his wrong side."

"Perhaps Emily found herself on his wrong side," I murmured. "If she was looking into a story about him and was close to the truth, he'd want her silenced. From the sound of things, she wasn't giving up until she found the information she needed."

"And if anyone was looking into Tommy's dodgy dealings, he'd have known about it," Bishop said. "The man has connections everywhere, and Emily wasn't always discreet when working on a new story."

"She could be a touch over-excitable," I said.

"Maybe that indiscretion got her killed," Ruby said.

"Have you spoken to Tommy?" Jacob asked Bishop. "Found out what he was doing on the night of the murder?"

"Not yet."

"We need to meet him," I said. "Get the measure of the man."

"That's the tricky thing. Tommy is hard to pin down. He has an army of assistants, and they always block the way. I was thinking about visiting his club this evening, though. He always puts in an appearance to do the rounds, shake hands, grease palms, that kind of thing."

"We'll come with you," I said. "We haven't made plans for this evening."

Bishop shuffled about in his seat. "It's not the kind of club for ladies. There are ladies there, but they're... working."

"Is it a brothel?" I asked.

"No! We wouldn't let that sort of thing go on," Bishop said. "It's best described as a... gentlemen's club. But the men aren't really gentlemen. It's hard to explain."

"We don't need you to explain it to us," I said. "We can see it for ourselves."

Bishop glanced at Jacob, and he shrugged. "When Veronica and Ruby set their minds to something, there's no deterring them. Is this club dangerous?"

After hesitating, Bishop shook his head. "Not as such. Things can get unruly, though. The men pay an inclusive fee to get into the club to watch the ladies dance. That fee covers an unlimited amount of alcohol—just the basic stuff—and then the girls entice the men to buy them expensive bottles of champagne to rack up debts. Tommy has fleeced a fair few holidaymakers using that tactic. They go in thinking all the drinks are free, and then the girls flutter their lashes to get them to cough up more money."

"We'll steer clear of ordering any champagne," I said. "What do you say, Ruby?"

Ruby smiled as she waved a chip in the air. "I say, let's go and see some ladies dancing."

Chapter 7

"Is Matthew not joining us this evening?" I settled in the dining room at our hotel with my mother and Jacob at a small, round table covered in a white linen cloth.

"He has a headache. He asked if he could have room service," my mother said with a hint of disdain.

I looked around the busy dining room as the wait staff dashed about. "While we're waiting for Ruby to arrive, I'll check on him. He's been doing so well, but with everything going on with Emily, it may be too much for him."

"I threatened to drag him out of bed, and he told me to leave him alone," my mother said. "It's not acceptable, hiding in his room and feigning an illness."

"Mother! You know Matthew never feigns. Look out for Ruby. I'll be back in a tick." I hurried out of the dining room and up the stairs to Matthew's bedroom. I knocked sharply on the door and waited a moment before it cracked open an inch.

Matthew's eye appeared in the space. "I have a headache. I've already ordered room service. I'm not coming down."

"How are you doing, old thing?" I asked. "I've been so busy today that I've barely seen you."

"Mother dragged me into three shops. It was too much. I couldn't take Felix in with me. He had to stand outside. He howled. I almost did too."

"She does her best, but she sometimes forgets your sensitive nature."

Matthew grunted. "Unable to fend for myself, like a weak Victorian fop too fond of his opium pipe, you mean?"

"I should have taken better care of you," I said.

"I survived. How are things going with Emily's investigation?" Matthew asked.

"We're gathering suspects. It would be marvellous if you lent a hand. You never know. You may have a knack for this sort of thing, and you could join Jacob in the new office."

He opened the door a little wider. "You're really going through with that plan?"

"Of course. Jacob approves and, providing we can find a suitable office space, we should be set up within two months."

"It's not for me," Matthew said.

"Wait." I gently pressed a hand against the door before he closed it. "Get some fresh air later when it's quiet. Felix will need a walk. Young dogs have so much energy."

"I will. I'll head to the beach."

"Jolly good. Just make sure to stay away from the pier." I said a quiet goodnight and walked away as Matthew closed the door. The poor chap was trying his best, but his struggle was real.

Just as I reached the bottom of the stairs, Ruby hurried into the lobby. "I know, I'm late."

"An Italian diversion?"

"Naturally. Alfonso wants to whisk me away for a weekend."

"You're already away for two weeks with me!"

"No, silly. To Italy." Ruby smoothed her hair.

"Whereabouts in Italy, exactly?"

"He told me a town name, but I can't remember how to pronounce it. How exciting, though. A man who likes adventure."

"Alfonso sounds too good to be true," I said. "It's high time we get a formal meeting underway."

"Don't you dare spoil my fun." Ruby glanced at my outfit. "Are you wearing that when we go to the club?"

"No! In case you forgot, we're dining with my mother before we leave. I've yet to tell her we're going out this evening. And they're waiting for us."

Ruby walked beside me as we returned to the dining room. "We should play it down to make sure she thinks it's an evening tea dance."

"They don't do tea dances in the evening," I said. "But you're right. She'll have an attack of the vapours if she knows what sort of club we're going to."

"I'm excited. It'll be nice to try something new."

"Just don't get excited talking about this evening. In fact, let me do the talking," I said. When I approached the table, I noticed we had a new dinner guest. Colonel Griffin had joined us.

He stood as we reached the table and pulled out chairs for both of us. "Good evening, ladies. I hope you don't mind, but Edith asked if I'd like to join you."

"Colonel Griffin was dining alone, and we can't have such a thing," my mother said.

"We're happy to have your company." And Colonel Griffin's presence would be the perfect distraction. My mother would be so busy talking to him that she may not question our evening activities too intensely.

"Bishop will be here in thirty minutes," Jacob murmured to me. "He's still not happy about taking us to the club, but he's secured us an entrance."

"That's all we need," I murmured back.

"I shall have the fish this evening," my mother declared.

"I've had enough fish for a few days," I said. "I'll go for something light. Quiche and salad, perhaps."

Once we'd placed our orders and enquired politely about each other's day, I decided it was time to bring up our venture out.

"Mother, I hope you won't object, but we thought we'd visit one of the dance halls this evening."

"Dancing! With my feet? Perish the thought."

"My dear lady, I imagine you cut a dash on the dance floor," Colonel Griffin said. "It would be my pleasure to accompany you. Of course, only if your daughter allows it."

My mother blushed and fluttered for a few seconds. "I'm charmed you think me capable of such a thing. But my dancing days are behind me. Since my husband departed this world, it's felt wrong to be too full of joy."

"Of course. A great loss for you," Colonel Griffin demurred.

"I was actually thinking of going with Jacob," I said as diplomatically as possible. "And he's bringing a friend for Ruby."

"The Maltese chap?" my mother asked.

"Alfonso is Italian," Ruby said. "But not him. It's a friend of Jacob's who lives here. Just to be my chaperone. After all, I can't stand on the sidelines and watch Jacob and Veronica enjoy themselves. That would be terribly dull."

"Will you be back late?" my mother asked.

"We won't be long," Jacob said. "My friend said it was an interesting venue and thought we might like a change of scene."

We all sat back as our food was served and then tucked straight in.

"What's the name of this dance hall?" Colonel Griffin asked. "I take a daily walk and like to nose around all the venues. Margate has such striking architecture. I'm astonished so much of it survived the air raids."

"It's at the far end of the amusements," Jacob said smoothly. "Have you been that way?"

"Ah! Not yet, but that gives me another target to find. I enjoyed a jolly good dance when I was a younger man. Can't do it now, of course. Although I'd give it a good try if Edith was amenable."

"Perhaps ten years ago I'd have been available for such a challenge," my mother said. "This fish is delicious."

The rest of the meal was passed in polite conversation, most of it between my mother and Colonel Griffin, and any attempts to discuss the evening dance were swiftly nipped in the bud.

Ruby nudged me. "You should change. You can borrow one of my outfits. I have plenty."

"Indeed, you do. You brought enough clothing for a month," I said.

"You look fine to me," Jacob said, "but you don't want to stand out for the wrong reasons."

I startled. "Do you mean I look plain?"

Jacob turned his attention to the last of his meal. Sensible choice.

"I'm slipping into my blue beaded number before we leave and freshening my makeup," Ruby said. "You should too. It'll only take five minutes."

I let out a gentle sigh. It wouldn't do to let the side down, so once we'd polished off our dinner, we made our excuses and headed upstairs. I endured Ruby fussing around me with her makeup, applying blush and powder to my cheeks before setting about my hair with so much vigour it made me yelp.

"Hush! You want to look your best for Jacob," she said.

"I want to look myself," I replied. "Not like a clown."

"I heard there were clowns at the local circus," Ruby said. "Alfonso knows them."

I caught hold of her hand. "Ruby, you aren't getting serious about this chap, are you? There's no harm in having fun, but I think it unlikely he'll whisk you into a world of romance in foreign lands."

"Even if it is all sweet-talking hot air, this is the fantasy I need. All I've had in my life recently are cads and rotters, and I'm done with it. Maybe a man from another country will know how to treat a lady," Ruby said with a wistful look.

"Just add a touch of caution to your interactions. I would hate for you to get into trouble."

"The only trouble coming our way is if Tommy catches us snooping around in his club," Ruby said. "What's the plan for tonight?"

"I'll let Bishop lead on this one," I said. "He has the local contacts."

"You won't be able to resist interfering, though." Ruby turned her attention to her face as I slipped into a more frivolous dress with a beaded hem.

"I'll direct when appropriate," I said. "Now hurry. By the time we get down, Bishop will have arrived."

"The gentlemen won't mind waiting," Ruby said. "After all, we are worth it."

By the time we returned to the main hotel lobby, Jacob and Bishop stood together chatting. I poked my head into the dining room and waved goodbye to my mother and Colonel Griffin, then we headed into the cool evening air and hailed a taxi. The fifteen-minute journey took us to a slightly rundown part of the amusements. We turned down a road, and the cabbie stopped outside a plain brick building. A large sign illuminated it, showing a dancing girl.

"Here's the club you're looking for. Seaside Delights. Are you sure you want to go in? It's not for the faint of heart," the cabbie cautioned, shooting a glance at Ruby and me.

"Quite sure." Bishop paid the cabbie, and we climbed out. Unfortunately, I'd had to leave Benji behind, but he was in excellent company with my brother and Felix.

"These women who dance, are they professionals?" I asked.

Bishop coughed into his hand. "They know how to work a room. And I should warn you, by the end of their performance, they aren't wearing many clothes."

"Burlesque striptease is so risqué!" Ruby said. "Most scandalous. Lead the way."

Bishop presented us at the entrance booth, showed our tickets, and we headed along a dark corridor towards jaunty music. As we stepped inside the main club, a mix of cheap perfume, ale, and heat hit me. The lighting was low, and a spotlight centred on a stage at the front. Everyone was sitting at tables. The majority of the clientele were men, although a number of women walked around them, selling cigarettes and cigars, and collecting drinks orders.

My attention turned to the stage, where a woman strutted around in a sparkly bra and knickers, with a large feather boa wrapped around her neck. "My goodness. She is terribly flexible."

"That's the star of the club." Bishop leaned close to be heard over the music. "Ivy Vance."

"Oh! I saw her at the opening of the new amusements," I said.

"I wish I could do the splits like that," Ruby said.

"Let's find a quiet booth at the back," Bishop suggested and led the way through the crowd. By the time we reached the booths, we could hear each other speak without raising our voices, and we settled into the leather seats.

A waitress came over to take our drinks order. Bishop stopped her before she left and placed money on her tray. "I need to speak to Tommy. It's police business. Tell him it's Bishop."

The woman barely raised an eyebrow as she nodded and tucked the money away before dashing off.

Five minutes later, our drinks arrived, and not far behind them was Tommy. He exuded a rough charm, dressed in a wide lapelled suit with his hair slicked back.

"Bishop! My man at the door told me you were in tonight. And you have friends with you." Tommy nodded a greeting at all of us as Bishop made the introductions. "I don't see you come around here too often."

"My friends wanted to get a flavour of the area," Bishop said.

"An authentic experience, you mean." Tommy chuckled. "You've come to the right place. I'm a born and bred Margate boy, so I can tell you everything there is to know about this town. It's the best seaside resort in the country. Not even those new package deals abroad can beat this. And we have the prettiest ladies, don't you think?" He winked at Ruby before his attention turned to the stage.

"We're not here for the entertainment," Bishop said. "Have you heard what happened to Emily Brewer?"

Tommy's expression sharpened. "I did. Fished out of the sea, wasn't she?"

"We believe she was pushed off the pier," I said. "Her death was no accident."

Tommy's reaction was one of surprise. He ran his hand through his hair several times then slid into the empty space in the booth. "How do you know that?"

"She had injuries," Bishop said.

"Emily fought with someone before she died?"

Bishop nodded. "We believe so."

Tommy stared off into space for a few seconds. "These young ones don't know how the world works. I told Emily to watch her back."

"Is that detailed in the complaint you filed about her?" I asked.

Jacob nudged me and shook his head.

"How would you know about that?" Tommy stiffened in his seat.

"Jacob and his friends are involved with the police in London," Bishop said. "And they're helping me figure out what happened to Emily."

"The old bill really is employing more women these days?" Tommy's gaze ran over me and Ruby. "I'm not sure I approve. Still, handy if you need to go undercover in a place like this. I can't imagine one of you fellows fitting in with a feather boa around your neck."

"What was your relationship with Emily?" I asked.

Tommy laid his hands flat on the table, his expression hard. "Don't come at me for this murder. I have a reputation, but I'm an honest man."

"I didn't say we were coming for you, but you caught Emily snooping on your private property. That must have angered you." My persistence earned me another hard nudge from Jacob.

Tommy glanced at the stage. "Emily was too nosy for her own good, and I had to chase her away from attempting to find dirt on me. I know what she was doing, sneaking about and looking in the dustbins, thinking I'd throw away a confidential letter or report that would get me in trouble. Here's the thing, there's no trouble on me. I got into a bit of mischief when

I was younger, but I run legitimate businesses. I'm a respectable man around Margate."

"Weren't you concerned Emily would come back and look for another story?" Bishop asked.

"At first, but then I realised she was an asset, so I hired her to snoop on my competitors."

"You did?" Bishop asked.

"Why have her working against me when I could pay her to work for me?" Tommy sat back in the booth. "And Emily did a top job. She helped me stop a rival company from buying a storefront I was interested in. She learned of their plans, and I gently persuaded them to look elsewhere."

"Terrified them away, you mean?" Bishop asked.

Tommy shook his head and chuckled. "I don't need to intimidate. I've got an excellent business reputation, and local people want to do business with me rather than strangers."

There was a raucous round of applause and plenty of wolf whistles as Ivy finished her set. She slid off the stage and headed straight towards our booth.

Tommy stood and kissed her on the cheek when she arrived. "Great show, darlin'. I've got a couple of councilmen at the back who want your special attention. Make sure you put a smile on their faces."

"In a moment, Tommy. What are you all talking about? It looked serious from the stage." Ivy's tone was low and husky, and now she was closer, I could tell she was young. Maybe just brushing twenty-five.

"This is just business. Nothing for you to worry about," Tommy said.

"Did Emily ever tell you she was writing a story about you?" I asked Tommy.

He waved away my words. "She wouldn't dare. I looked out for her. She helped me, so I helped her. It was tit-for-tat."

"To keep your name out of this investigation, you won't mind telling me where you were on the night Emily was murdered," Bishop said.

Ivy took a step back, a flash of surprise crossing her face. "I've been hearing the rumours. Emily was definitely killed?"

I nodded, my attention shifting to Ivy. Did she know anything about this situation? "What rumours have you heard?"

Tommy huffed a breath. "Don't bother my girls. Ivy knows nothing."

Ivy pursed her lips but remained silent.

"Don't let it bother you, darlin'. The police are poking around. You know what they're like." Tommy gently pushed Ivy away. "Go and see those councilmen before they get annoyed. And as for my alibi, I was at the club all night. You can check with half a dozen of my staff."

"We may do that," Bishop said. "Just to be certain."

"Knock yourself out. Ivy, I told you to go." Tommy's tone turned frosty.

"I just want to say hello to my favourite man." Ivy stepped forward and pressed a lingering kiss on Bishop's cheek. I didn't miss that she pressed something into his hand before stepping back. "Enjoy your evening, everybody." She waltzed off.

"I need to go, too. Plenty of people to see. And the drinks are on me. Whatever you like." Tommy strolled away.

The second he was gone, Bishop opened the note Ivy had given him. It read: *Usual place. Midnight.*

Chapter 8

"When Ivy said she wanted to meet at your usual place, I thought she meant a discreet guesthouse." I tried not to shiver as we stood under Margate Pier on the damp sand, waiting for Ivy to arrive. My wristwatch had just ticked past the midnight hour.

"It's not that kind of relationship," Bishop said. He stood beside Jacob, Ruby next to him.

"Ivy seemed overly familiar with you in the club," Ruby said. "Are you close?"

"Close enough to know not to get romantically entangled with the likes of Ivy Vance," Bishop replied.

Benji woofed a soft bark as if in agreement. I'd collected him from the hotel before coming here to meet Ivy with the others. Matthew had left him with my mother for company, rather than taking him on a walk with Felix. I didn't blame him. When the dogs were together, they could be boisterous.

"If your relationship isn't romantic, what is it?" Ruby clutched her thin jacket around her shoulders.

"Perhaps the kind that shouldn't be probed too deeply in case it causes trouble." Jacob leaned against a wooden pier strut. Although he'd never admit it, he was tired.

It had been a busy day, and I'd not given him enough chance to rest. Of course, if I'd attempted to get him to take things easy, he'd have accused me of fussing.

"I've known Ivy ever since I came down to Kent," Bishop said.

"Did you meet her in the club?" Ruby asked.

"I don't go there when I have time off," Bishop said. "It's not my sort of thing. We literally bumped into each other on the promenade. She dropped her ice cream on my suit jacket and insisted she clean it. In return, I bought her a new ice cream, and we got talking. Ivy has a heart of gold. When she can help, she does."

"In your investigations?" I asked. "Is she an informant?"

"Hush now. Use words like that and people find themselves dead," Bishop warned. "All I'll say is that Ivy is one of Tommy's favourites, and she often overhears things she shouldn't. Tommy trusts her not to talk, so he sometimes lets secrets slip out."

"But she talks to you," Ruby said. "Are you sure she has no ulterior motives? You'd be a catch for many a woman."

A small smile played across Bishop's lips, but he shook his head. "A fine lady like Ivy would eat me alive and spit out the mangled pieces. We have a professional relationship. Besides, Ivy likes her men much richer than I'll ever be."

"I didn't realise I'd be attending a party." Ivy's voice sounded close, making me jump. She'd crept across the sand without any of us seeing or hearing her.

"Sorry, Ivy, but they're involved in Emily's case," Bishop said. "And we think you may be able to help."

"Not with an audience." Ivy turned away. "The only time I enjoy being among a crowd is when I'm performing and getting well paid for it."

"Please, don't go," I said. "I knew Emily. That's what you want to talk to us about, isn't it?"

Ivy hesitated. "What do you know about her?"

"I know her Aunt Mabel. I own the Harbour Arms and met Emily a number of times when I visited on business."

Ivy turned back to us, her gaze sharp. "I always appreciate meeting another professional woman. It's still a rare thing, even in these modern times. How did you come by the pub?"

"My father acquired a portfolio of pubs, which passed to me when he died. We came down to help with Jacob's recuperation." I pointed at his leg. "And to catch up on business at the Harbour Arms."

"Mixing business with pleasure. That can be a heady combination," Ivy said. "I often learn my most interesting facts under the guise of pleasure."

"You can trust them," Bishop said. "Jacob used to work for the police in London. Veronica and Ruby often helped with his investigations."

"My! You have many feathers in your cap." Ivy's expression grew appraising. "Very well. I trust Bishop, so if he believes you're sensible, then so do I. But if I find myself in trouble, I'll know who to visit. Believe me, you won't enjoy that visit."

"We'll be discreet," I said. "What can you tell us about Emily?"

"We didn't run in the same circles, but I knew her. She was sweet. Some people can be terribly judgemental of my lifestyle choices, but not Emily."

"Do you know what happened to her?" I asked.

Ivy's gaze slid to the dark waves behind us. "This information doesn't come for free. I make myself vulnerable every time I deal with Bishop."

"You'll get your payment," Bishop assured her.

"I want two bottles of gin. And some of that new Chanel perfume. Not a small bottle."

"Gosh. That's not cheap," Ruby said. "I've been eyeing it myself, but my wage won't stretch to it."

"Mine will, but why pay for something when you can get a man to buy it for you?" Ivy smirked. "I'm sure a pretty face like yours can easily secure a handsome husband if you so desire. Although I believe husbands are more trouble than they're worth. It's why I prefer other women's husbands. Far less complicated."

"Tell us what you know about Emily," Bishop said.

Ivy slunk under the pier, so she was well out of sight of anyone wandering along the beach at such a late hour. "To get you all up to speed, Tommy considers me his special girl. It's my role in his club. I lead the dance troupe, always have the top spot during performances, and offer my services to a number of influential private clients."

"In exchange for payment?" I asked.

"I don't undervalue my talents. And I have many. My clients leave well satisfied and with empty pockets. It works for both of us."

I nodded. It wasn't my place to judge, but I couldn't imagine it being a profession Ivy enjoyed. Although it was clear her services were highly prized. Diamonds glinted in her earlobes, and she had a matching bracelet around one wrist.

"Ivy excels in getting her clients talking," Bishop said, gesturing for her to continue.

"They love their pillow talk," Ivy said. "We conduct our business, and when they're relaxed, enjoying a glass of wine or a brandy and a cigarette, they offload their troubles. Sometimes, it's dull information about their businesses or a local political event. But many of my gentlemen have investments in Margate. Investments that perhaps weren't obtained through legal means."

"What about Tommy?" Jacob asked. "If you work for him, aren't you loyal to him?"

"Sweetheart, I'm only loyal to myself," Ivy said. "I trust myself implicitly. The same can't be said for anybody else. I've learned through hard experience that people are quick to let you down when a new opportunity comes along."

"Heartbreak?" I asked.

"My heart is too hard to be broken these days," Ivy said. "But if you don't mind, let's not talk about me."

"My apologies," I said. "Please, go on."

"I find it useful to listen to Tommy's private conversations, too," Ivy said. "He trusts me as best he can, so I'm rarely excluded when he conducts business. If I'm around and the conversation is stimulating, I make myself useful while taking note of anything of interest."

"Did Tommy have a problem with Emily?" I asked.

Ivy scowled, her gaze flicking back to the churning waves. "I still can't believe what happened to her. The trouble with Emily was she could never keep quiet. When she fixated on a story or thought she'd found something scandalous, she kept digging, questioning, going after anyone, regardless of their position in society."

"Do you know if Tommy went after Emily because she wouldn't leave him alone?" I held my breath, waiting for an answer.

Ivy crossed her arms over her chest. "I recently heard Tommy complaining about Emily. He'd underestimated her strength of character. He thought she was a silly girl he could win over, and assumed if he was paying her, she'd stop looking into him."

"Tommy told us Emily investigated a business rival for him," I said.

"That's true. Emily was excellent at what she did, and her tenacious nature rarely failed to find the facts to expose an injustice. My theory is that tenacity led to her downfall," Ivy said. "And Emily turned the tables on Tommy. Once she had her foot in the door, she refused to budge."

"What was she investigating Tommy for?" Bishop asked.

"Emily believed Tommy uses the club for money laundering," Ivy said. "He made the mistake of leaving Emily in his office on one occasion. When he got back, he caught her rifling through his papers. He was so angry, he threw her out of the club himself. Lifted her clean off the floor and carried her outside."

Jacob looked at Bishop. "Have you ever tried to catch Tommy out on money laundering charges?"

"I know there's something dodgy about the way he makes his money, but his books have been inspected. I don't know how he cooks them, but they're squeaky clean," Bishop said.

"Do you know about the money laundering?" I asked Ivy.

"I stay out of that side of things," Ivy said. "I collect information when I can, but I know which side my bread is buttered. My focus is on my high-powered clients. They're my long-term ticket to success. I don't plan on being a dancer for many more years, so I'll be leaving Tommy behind when a more suitable target opens up."

"You're looking for a man to support your lifestyle?" Ruby asked. "I'd like one of those, but the well-heeled men with deep pockets I stumble across usually have few teeth, bleary vision, and terrible breath."

Ivy chuckled. "I hear you there. If I don't find a suitable horse to attach my wagon to, I'll rely on my own success. Working for Tommy pays well, and my private clients do the same, so it won't be much longer. After all, a woman can only perform the splits so many times before something breaks."

"You've got plenty of good years in you if you choose to stay dancing," Bishop said. "We'd miss you around Margate, if you left."

Ivy uncrossed her arms and gently patted Bishop's cheek. "If only you were wealthier. You're handsome enough for me."

"Getting back to Emily," I said, "what did Tommy say to her when they argued?"

The smile slipped from Ivy's face. "He lost control. He rarely raises his voice, but he was bellowing at her."

"That suggests Emily found something she shouldn't," Bishop said.

"It could be that, although it could also be that Tommy was disappointed at being tricked," I said. "Emily bruised Tommy's ego, and he wanted her to pay."

"I was hidden at the back of the club, but I heard every word Tommy yelled," Ivy said. "I didn't hear Emily's reply, but Tommy threatened her. He said he'd make her sorry."

"Emily wasn't the sort to back down, even when threatened," I said. "She wouldn't have walked away if she thought there was a story."

"So Tommy silenced her," Jacob said. "What about his alibi? He said he was at the club on the night of the murder."

"Did you see Tommy that night?" I asked Ivy.

"He was there some of the time. I performed with my ladies. We did three group numbers and then the solo performances. I was finished around eleven, got changed in the dressing room, and then went to a private party. I must have got there no later than eleven-thirty."

"Emily wasn't killed until after midnight," Bishop said. "We'll need to check the club to see if Tommy was there that late."

"He's always popping in and out," Ivy said. "He uses the club to conduct business, and he also invites influential people in to butter them up if he's got plans for them."

"How long does the club stay open?" Jacob asked.

"It's supposed to close at midnight," Bishop said.

"Yes, it's supposed to, isn't it?" Ivy smirked again. "The music is turned down at midnight, and the doors are locked, but there are often private parties going on until the early hours of the morning."

"I'll do some digging," Bishop said. "I'll return to the club in the morning and find out who was working there, see if anyone saw Tommy at that time or if he was spotted sneaking off."

Ivy clutched Bishop's arm. "I know you're aware of this, but be careful of Tommy. He pretends he's respectable, but he's dangerous. He's chased a number of business rivals out of town by ruining them. He's not beyond ending someone's life if they're stopping him from getting what he wants."

"Which is what he could have done to Emily," I said.

Ivy drew in a sharp breath. "If Tommy killed Emily, I won't work with him anymore. I have hard lines, and when they're crossed, that's it. No woman should lose her life because she's exposing problems."

"I'll be careful," Bishop said. "But you must promise to do the same. You're around Tommy more than I am. He can't learn you're helping me."

Ivy stepped forward and pressed a kiss on his cheek. "We've been doing this dance a long time, and he hasn't learned about it yet. Tommy thinks he has me under his thumb, when the truth is I have him completely captivated. It's my shimmy, you see." She gave us a little demonstration.

Bishop chuckled. "Promise me."

"Very well. I'll be extra cautious. And if I hear new information, you'll be the first to know. All of you." With that, Ivy turned and slipped away into the night as silently as she'd arrived.

Jacob blew out a breath. "It's looking likely Tommy killed Emily. If we can pull his alibi apart, we've got our man."

Ruby briskly rubbed her arms. "Let's go back to the hotel. I'm about to perish on this beach. This chill breeze doesn't feel like it's summer."

We all agreed it was too cold to remain there a second longer, so we trudged away from the pier. We'd only taken a few steps before there was a cry for help.

Benji's ears pricked, and he looked towards the waves.

"Where did that come from?" Ruby was looking around. "That was a man's voice, wasn't it?"

"Is that someone in the water? What blithering fool would take a midnight swim?" Bishop was striding towards the sea, but Benji outpaced him and had already dived in.

The cry came again, and my heart leapt into my throat. "That was Matthew!"

Chapter 9

I raced to the water's edge, following Benji and Bishop into the freezing, salty waves. I didn't glance over my shoulder as I left Jacob and Ruby trailing after me. I couldn't worry about them. My foolish brother was in trouble.

Icy saltwater soaked my hosiery and hem as I waded through the waves. I was grateful for the shallow waters and gentle slope into the deeper sea. My breath had been stolen from me in the panic of the situation.

"I've got him in my sights!" Bishop yelled as he saw me following. "Go back to the shore. I don't want you getting in trouble, too."

I ploughed on. I was a capable swimmer, and it was my brother in peril, so I didn't intend to stand idly by.

"Felix is with him!" Jacob called from the sand.

Sure enough, when I squinted through the dark, I caught a flash of Felix's fur as he paddled around Matthew, who flailed about and went under, one arm wrapped around Felix. By now, Bishop was almost to him, as was Benji. With a sickening lurch, they dove under the water at the same time as Matthew disappeared, all swallowed in the murky depths.

Benji emerged first. He was on his own. He splashed around, searching for Matthew, before vanishing under the waves again.

My heart pounded a frantic rhythm in my ears as the terrifying scene unfolded. A fleeting glimpse of Felix's fur caught my eye, a stark contrast against the churning, dark water. He was desperately paddling before going under again.

Seconds stretched into what felt like hours as I scanned the surface, my eyes desperate for any sign of movement. A flash of white - Felix? No, just a cruel trick of the light. The water was a menacing, indifferent abyss, swallowing up everything in its path.

Then, a furry head broke the surface. It was Benji, and he had hold of Matthew's collar. Bishop appeared a second later with Felix. A wave of relief washed over me, so intense it was almost painful.

There were a few seconds of struggle and spluttering as my hero dog and Bishop brought Matthew and Felix back to the sand. I followed, my pulse racing so fast I thought I might pass out.

"Whatever were you doing in there? You almost drowned!" I was caught between anger and terror and took my frustrations out on Matthew with a swipe of my hand against his shoulder.

He coughed a few times, crouched on the beach next to Felix, both of them drenched and shivering. "I had no choice! Felix went into the water, and he wouldn't come out, no matter how much I yelled. I tried everything, but he kept swimming farther. If I hadn't gone after him, I'd have lost him."

"Didn't you have him on his lead?" My anger faded. Of course, my brother would go in to rescue his beloved dog. Felix meant the world to him.

"I thought we'd be fine without it. There was no one around, and Felix has so much energy that a good run along the beach would help him burn it off. I think he saw something in the water, and off he went."

"When we get back to London, it's more training for young Felix." I gently patted Matthew's shoulder, all forgiven. But for a second, I'd thought the worst. When Matthew had returned from his service during the Great War, he'd experienced dark thoughts, and I'd feared for his life. When I'd seen him in trouble in the water, all those old concerns had flared up.

"You poor old thing," Ruby said to Matthew. "You're freezing and drenched. Let's get you back to the hotel so you can dry off. And Veronica, shame on you. You've ruined my dress!"

I winced as I looked at the sand encrusted, sodden garment. "In the panic, I didn't think. I'll buy you a new one."

Ruby grinned. "You're forgiven. Besides, I was thinking about donating it to charity. I'm just glad Matthew and Felix are fine."

Bishop stood next to Jacob, dripping onto the sand. "If you're not used to these waters, the currents will surprise you. It's most likely your dog got caught up in a riptide and couldn't get free."

"It seemed to me he was intent on paddling to the horizon. Thank you for the help. I wasn't going to leave him, but I was running out of energy." Matthew glanced at me. "I knew going outside was a bad idea."

We returned to the hotel to dry off. Jacob stopped as I got to my door. He'd barely said a word during our walk back to the hotel. "I'm sorry I couldn't help."

"We had everything under control," I said. "And with a damaged leg, I could hardly expect you to play the hero. Besides, I usually have that role ably covered."

He looked down at his leg. "Dratted injury. I feel useless. I limp around all day, slowing you down, and making you worry because I may be in pain."

"I have every reason to worry." My expression softened at his careworn face. "I... I don't dislike you. You're acceptable to be around, so I decide you stay with me, no matter how slowly you walk. We walk together."

Jacob's eyebrow arched. "Do I get a say on that matter?"

"Absolutely not. Well, maybe a small amount, when I'm in the right mood." I touched his elbow. "All you need is time and patience. And all everyone else needs is a good night's sleep. Today has been quite an adventure. I didn't expect it to end taking a midnight swim to save my brother and his misbehaving pup."

"It's never dull when you're around." Jacob nodded. "And tomorrow, it all begins again."

After a hearty breakfast of kippers and toast with my mother, I headed up to Matthew's room with a tray of breakfast I'd requested from the kitchen and knocked on the door.

"It's open," he called out.

I headed inside with toast, soft-boiled eggs, and tea for him. He was huddled under blankets, looking very sorry for himself. Felix lay at the end of the bed, wagging his tail when he saw me, as if he hadn't been the cause of so much chaos just a short time ago.

"How are you feeling after last night's dip?" I set the tray down for Matthew.

He gave an enormous sneeze. "I have a cold. I'm staying here today."

"Try to get out if you can. I know last night was a shocker, but don't let one setback upset all your hard work. You have enjoyed yourself so far, haven't you?" I patted Felix and gently nudged him away from the food.

"It's not been terrible. But I wish I was back home." Matthew sneezed again. "It's all so stimulating. The noise and people. I don't know how you do it every day."

"It's because you're not used to it," I said. "It'll get better the more you get involved. I know it's tricky, but you're making good progress. And I've never seen our mother smile so much."

"She is enjoying herself," Matthew said. "I don't think she's mentioned her racing heart more than a dozen times since we arrived."

"That's because she mentioned it so frequently on our way down that she used up her weekly allowance."

Matthew chuckled. "Sorry for messing around last night. I really was trying to save Felix."

"I'd have done the same for Benji," I said. "But you did worry me."

"I know. You didn't say anything, but I saw it in your eyes." Matthew reached for my hand and gave it a brief squeeze. "I'm past all that. I may never be fully healed—some things you never recover from—but I am better than I was. And I want to be better for you and Mother."

"And for yourself," I said.

He shrugged. "And Felix. Do you want to take him today? He'll go stir-crazy stuck in this room with me while I'm sneezing and trying to get rid of the sand still stuck in every crevice."

"That's an excellent idea. We're off to look at more offices for the new business."

"Have a fun day." Matthew lay back and munched on a piece of toast, more relaxed now he knew I wasn't pressing him into any new adventures.

After I'd collected Jacob, Benji, and Ruby, I headed out onto the street, Felix on a close lead beside me. I'd make sure there were no more jollies in the sea while he was by my side.

"I'm excited about this new adventure of yours." Ruby strolled along, wearing a fashionably high waisted dress in a delicate shade of salmon pink. "Having a seaside bolthole will be perfect. I could come down most weekends."

"It's a business, not a bolthole," Jacob said.

"Your friend could show me around if you're too busy." Ruby dodged a beady-eyed seagull.

Jacob shook his head. "Bishop also works."

"Won't your new Italian companion keep you company when you visit Margate?" I asked.

"Alfonso works a lot, too. And he travels, so I can't guarantee he'll always be around. And I need a capable chap to show me the sights."

"Entertain you, you mean," I said.

"If Bishop is free, I'm sure he'll escort you," Jacob said.

"Ruby is perfectly capable of escorting herself," I said.

She thumped my arm and gasped. "Oh, my! There he is! What a delightful surprise. I'll see you later back at the hotel." With barely a goodbye, Ruby dashed off into Alfonso's arms.

I sighed at their overt display of affection, which caused several older couples to shake their head in disapproval.

"You don't like Alfonso?" Jacob asked.

"I'm concerned this blossoming relationship may end badly," I said. "Ruby wears her heart on her sleeve and falls in love almost immediately. I don't want this chap to take advantage and then scurry back to Italy, leaving me to hunt for the pieces of Ruby's shattered heart."

"Ruby is a capable woman," Jacob said. "If he messes her around, she'll give him what for."

"And I'll be right beside her when she does."

A few moments later, we arrived at our first office viewing and were met by a cheerful agent who showed us around the premises. It was much smaller and darker than the photographs we'd been sent and was dismissed because of an obvious damp problem.

The second office had potential and included a partial sea view. After exploring the small kitchenette, I returned to the main office. "Think about all the people we can help by opening this business."

Jacob nodded. "There's plenty of potential. And I'm definitely warming to the idea of being in business with you."

While the agent went up the stairs, fiddling with the keys to open the living quarters, I caught hold of Jacob's hand. "Are you really? I was worried you'd think it was foolish, but you have the perfect skills to make this business a success."

"As do you. You could open it without me."

"There'd be no fun in that," I said. "And a woman only has so many hours in a day. Looking after my family, managing the pubs, the newspaper, and now this. I'd keel over with exhaustion like a Victorian waif."

Jacob edged closer. "I'll be here to catch you if you fall."

I blinked in surprise as his head lowered to mine. Was this the romance Jacob had been attempting to discuss with me? Was his plan to show me his feelings rather than lay his romantic cards on the table?

Felix barged his way between us, wagging his tail and jumping up at Jacob.

I laughed and stepped back. The moment passed, and the agent appeared to show us the living quarters, giving me time to settle my pulse and compose myself. I admired Jacob, but my feelings were buttoned up. If we changed our relationship, things would never be the same again. Did I want that? A part of me did.

"This has potential," I said as we left the viewing. "How about we take a break? I want to buy some sticks of rock for Matthew."

Jacob checked his wristwatch. "We have time. I'm meeting Bishop later to see what he's learned about Tommy."

"From what we're discovering about that man, the situation looks bad for him," I said.

"We just need the evidence to prove he murdered Emily."

"Let's stop at the Harbour Arms on the way," I said. "I keep meaning to check on Mabel."

The pub was only a ten-minute walk from the office. It wasn't yet open for business, but the barrel man was carrying in ale, so the front door was wide open. We stepped through the doorway and discovered Mabel behind the bar. When she saw me, she dashed over, looking flustered and angry.

"Is there another problem?" I asked.

"I've been going through Emily's things," Mabel said. "And I found a threatening note!"

"A note?" Jacob glanced at me. "What does it say?"

"I've got it here. I couldn't believe it when I found it." Mabel headed around the bar and handed over a crumpled note. The handwriting was messy and barely legible.

"Stay out of my business if you know what's good for you," Jacob read. "When did Emily receive this?"

"I don't know! She never told me about it." Mabel was breathless with anger. "I was getting together notebooks for Veronica when I discovered it. That's our killer! Whoever wrote that threat is the murderer."

"There could be a connection to what happened to Emily." There was a note of caution in Jacob's voice. "Bishop will need to see this. I'm meeting him soon."

"Whoever sent it wasn't brave enough to put their name on it," I said. "What a cowardly move."

"If I knew who it was, I'd let them have it," Mabel said. "How dare they threaten Emily. She was only young. She was trying to do her job, and this is what happens."

I carefully studied the note, turning over the crumpled paper. "I only know of one profession that tolerates such untidy handwriting. And you see here, these marks pressed into the paper. Mabel, have you got a pencil?"

She looked behind the bar for a few seconds, then handed me a pencil. I pressed it lightly against the paper, shading in the indentations. "I see part of what might be a name. P-A-T. Could it be Doctor Patterson?"

We all inspected the marks.

"It makes no sense why he'd be involved," Mabel said. "He's a charming man and so good with the young people. You often see him with them. They call him Doctor Helpful."

"But you saw Emily and Doctor Patterson arguing," I said. "And when we questioned him about it, he claimed it was because he stepped on Emily's foot and annoyed her."

Mabel's brow furrowed. "That doesn't sound right to me. Emily wouldn't get angry over something so small."

"Bishop needs to know about this note immediately," Jacob said.

"You contact Bishop," I said. "And I'll go to Doctor Patterson's house and see if he's home."

"Don't confront him." Jacob was already heading to the door. "If he murdered Emily, he may not come quietly. You could find yourself in trouble."

"Then you'd better hurry to the police station and collect your friend," I said.

After a brief second of hesitation, Jacob dashed away.

I turned to Mabel. "What does Doctor Patterson talk to the young people about?"

"I can't say for certain," Mabel said. "He's a friendly man. I always thought he was giving them guidance or free advice on how to look after themselves. Some young people have no sense of danger and get into all kinds of muddles."

That sounded suspicious. Doctor Patterson wasn't a young man and should mingle with his own peers, not spend time with young, impressionable people.

"You keep this note safe," I said to Mabel. "Jacob and Bishop won't be long."

"I could come with you," Mabel said. "I don't want you getting into any trouble."

"I have two fearsome dogs and an efficient right hook should the need arise," I said.

"I've no doubt you can look after yourself." Mabel looked up as the ale man reappeared with another barrel.

"And you have your hands full here," I said. "I'll make no accusations. Simply see what the good doctor is up to and ask him about Emily again. Perhaps he's had time to come up with a more convincing lie than the last time we met."

After making reassurances with Mabel, I hurried out of the pub and headed to Doctor Patterson's house. When I reached the front door, I knocked several times, but no one answered. I walked around the back and found a door slightly ajar, so I peeked inside. There was no sign of Doctor Patterson, but his wife, Patricia, was asleep in a comfortable armchair, a blanket over her knees.

I stepped into the room, and she roused. "Hello. Do you remember me? I paid your husband a visit recently. Veronica Vale."

Patricia feebly lifted a hand and blinked at me, her eyes taking a few seconds to focus. "I think so. Are you here to give me my medication?"

"No, I'll leave that in your husband's capable hands." I walked closer. She was pale, and there was a slight tremor in her hand. "I'm so sorry you're unwell. Does your illness affect your memory?"

"I always feel confused," Patricia said. "My husband looks after me, though. He gives me everything I need."

"It's a good job you're married to a doctor," I said. "Medicine on tap."

She nodded and blinked slowly. "I ... yes. A good thing. I'm lucky."

"Have you heard the bad news about Emily?" I asked gently.

"I'm not sure. Was she injured?"

"Unfortunately, she was found drowned," I said. "Did you know her?"

"Oh! Yes, I remember now. My husband told me what happened. Poor child."

I helped her lift a glass of water to her lips.

"Thank you. Where is my husband?"

"I'm sure he won't be far away," I said.

"No, he always looks after me." Patricia closed her eyes and sighed.

"Do you remember two nights ago? The night Emily died. Can you remember where your husband was?"

"Most likely here, wasn't he? I don't know for sure. I lose track of time, you see. But he never abandons me. I sometimes think he should. Who wants a sick wife?"

"He loves you," I said. "He wants to look after you."

"Yes, we protect our marriage vows," she said. "In sickness and in health."

"We always care for the ones we love, even when they're sick."

"It's a burden."

"It's kindness."

Patricia fell silent.

"Do you recall the night the new amusements opened?" I asked. "There was a big party in town and your husband stepped out to attend. Do you remember that?"

Patricia drew in a breath. "I do. They had fireworks. I heard those."

"I believe so," I said. "How long did your husband leave you that night?"

Patricia sighed again. "I'm sorry. I'm no use to anyone."

The living room door swung open, and Doctor Patterson stood there, anger on his face. "What the devil is going on here?"

Chapter 10

I stepped back from Patricia, noticing Benji's hackles had raised the second Doctor Patterson appeared, irritation radiating from him. Felix was discreetly chewing on a slipper he'd discovered tucked under a chair, oblivious to the tension.

"I was just having a pleasant conversation with your wife. I hope you don't mind, but I let myself in," I said.

Doctor Patterson stormed into the room. "I jolly well do mind. This is my home, and you're trespassing."

"The back door was open," I said. "I saw no harm in coming in and speaking with Patricia. I thought she might be lonely on her own or get confused when she woke. Where were you?"

"That's none of your damned business." Doctor Patterson crouched beside Patricia. "Is this woman pestering you?"

Patricia looked at me for several long seconds and then turned to her husband. "Do we know her?"

"No, we don't. And she was just leaving," Doctor Patterson said. "It's unfair to pester a sick woman."

"I wasn't pestering," I said. "I was keeping her company. Which is more than you were doing."

"I heard your questions. When I came in the front door and there was an unfamiliar voice in the house, I stopped to listen. You were interrogating Patricia about my whereabouts on the night of Emily's murder. How dare you think I had anything to do with it."

"We're looking to eliminate as many suspects as quickly as possible," I said. "We must get to the bottom of this matter."

"I'm disgusted you think I could be a suspect. I barely knew Emily."

"I'm not sure I believe you," I said. "I've been hearing how you spend your time with the younger people in town. What was the appeal with Emily?"

"No appeal! And I don't like your insinuation," Doctor Patterson said. "Emily wasn't a friend of this household."

"She was an enemy?"

"No! I won't allow you to twist my words," Doctor Patterson said. "We barely knew Emily. I was aware she was a bright and ambitious young woman who wanted to be a journalist, but that's about it. I'm too busy with my duties here to fuss around someone young enough to be my daughter."

"You never spoke to Emily when you spent time with her friends?" I asked. "Remind me again what you spoke to them about?"

"That is none of your concern." Doctor Patterson's face was bright red. "I shall make a complaint about you. You're upsetting a grievously ill woman for no reason other than to poke about like a curious cat into things that have nothing to do with you."

Benji growled again, and this time, Felix joined in, both dogs sensing the rising tension.

"And keep those beasts away from me and my wife," Doctor Patterson said. "I'll have them put down if they so much as sniff Patricia."

"We'll be having more than words if you harm one fur on these dogs' heads," I said. "You're being defensive and unnecessarily obtuse. Why not answer my questions if you have nothing to conceal?"

"Because you're a troublemaker who refuses to leave," Doctor Patterson said. "My wife is ill!"

"So you keep saying," I said. "But I'm not here to bother her. I came here to ask you about a note you sent Emily."

Doctor Patterson's eyes widened. "I don't know what you're talking about. Why would I send a note to a person I don't know?"

"Emily? Did you say Emily was here?" Patricia roused in her seat. "I thought she was dead. Didn't I hear that?"

"Pay no attention to Miss Vale. She's hysterical," Doctor Patterson said. "Emily wouldn't visit us."

"I'm hysterical? Is that your professional diagnosis?" I asked. "Are you about to have me committed to an asylum because I won't keep quiet and dutiful?"

"You have a nerve! You bother me and you upset my fragile wife," Doctor Patterson snapped. "You're making baseless accusations, and I won't have it."

"The way you keep focusing on your sick wife makes me think you're deflecting to gain sympathy," I said.

"I'm deflecting nothing. And it's time you left," he insisted.

"We don't like Emily." Patricia's gaze focused on me. "Emily is sour."

Doctor Patterson hurriedly caressed his wife's hand in a movement that was supposed to be calming but seemed swift and terse. "You're getting confused. It's almost time for your next dose of medicine."

"You said she was a journalist," Patricia said to him. "That's the one we don't like, isn't it? The nosy, proud one who talks too much."

"No, you're making a mistake." Doctor Patterson glanced at me. "You've got yourself worked up because of this intruder. I should have you arrested for this."

"I'm close to Emily's Aunt Mabel," I said to Patricia, "and I knew Emily. I will get to the bottom of what happened to her."

"Not from us. We had nothing to do with her death," Doctor Patterson said.

"Then why write Emily a threatening note?" I asked. "The terrible handwriting suggests a doctor wrote it. And you made the mistake of using a notepad you'd written your name on. The impression was on the page you left for Emily to find."

Doctor Patterson appeared frozen, one hand tight on his wife's shoulder as he glared at me.

"It was you, wasn't it?" I persisted. "You warned Emily away. The threat was clear. I take it she ignored you, so you taught her a lesson. What happened? Did you arrange to meet at the pier and she refused to back down? In your anger, you pushed her?"

"Emily is rude and obnoxious," Patricia said.

"Not now, my love," Doctor Patterson muttered. "Perhaps I need to alter your dosage. You shouldn't be this confused so early in the day."

"If you both disliked Emily, there must be a reason," I said. "Did she find out something about you?"

"No! Because there's nothing underhand to find out about either of us," Doctor Patterson said. "We live a quiet life. We always have done. Even when based in London, our world was ordinary. I worked, and Patricia kept the house. Some may say it was a boring life, but it suited us."

"I didn't realise you moved from London," I said. "That's quite a change. Coming from the hustle of urban living to a town designed for tourists. Do you not find the winters here dull?"

"It was a long-overdue move," Doctor Patterson said. "As Patricia's health declined, I realised I needed to take things easier. For a while, life was balanced, but she became even more unwell, so the practice took a back seat. It was for the best."

"So, it wasn't your business practices that Emily investigated?" I asked. "An affair?"

Doctor Patterson sucked in a breath. "Do not speak of such disgraceful things in front of my wife. She's easily confused and can get the wrong ideas in her head. If you're not careful, you'll have her believing I was unfaithful."

"Perhaps you were, and Emily discovered the truth," I said. "She thought you should tell your wife, and you didn't approve. Is that what your fight was over?"

"You are unbelievably stubborn," Doctor Patterson said.

"I'm determined to get to the truth," I said. "There's a difference. Was Emily concerned about the amount of time you spend with younger people?"

"Oh, I do so like their visits. All our young friends stopping by." Patricia looked up at me. "We have no children, but we like to help the young ones."

"Hush now," Doctor Patterson said. "Miss Vale doesn't need to hear about that."

"I very much do," I said. "You have a younger crowd coming here? Surely, that must be a strain on you."

"It's no bother, and they don't stay for long," Patricia said. "They come to the door, speak to my husband, and leave."

I furrowed my brow. "Why do that? Do you have such extensive knowledge that you can advise the local youth on their varied problems?"

"I was a respected Scout group leader in London, so I have experience with young people. Not that it's your concern," Doctor Patterson said.

"It is strange, though," I said. "Did Emily ever visit you for advice?"

"We would never let her in," Patricia said. "She was such an unpleasant creature."

"My dear, Emily is dead," Doctor Patterson murmured. "You must speak kindly about her."

"But she yelled! She was mean to you."

Doctor Patterson's gaze flicked to me. "You're thinking about somebody else."

Patricia massaged her forehead. "Am I? Who was shouting at you in the garden?"

"No one. Now, be quiet. I think we'll have an early dose of your medicine as soon as Miss Vale leaves, and then you can take a long nap. The stress is unsettling you." Doctor Patterson gestured towards the exit, but I wasn't ready to leave.

Before I could continue my questioning, there was a knock at the front door, causing Doctor Patterson to sigh. "Now what? Why can't we be left on our own?"

"Perhaps it's one of your young friends, looking for advice," I said as sweetly as possible.

"No, they only come twice a week, when they're supposed to," Patricia said.

"Don't say another word. I'll get the door." Doctor Patterson dashed away and returned a few seconds later with Jacob and Bishop. They both looked serious. "I'm glad you're here. I have a trespasser on my property, and she's refusing to leave."

"Veronica is with us," Jacob said.

"I don't know you," Doctor Patterson said.

"Veronica and Jacob are helping me to investigate Emily's death," Bishop said. "And I've just been inspecting evidence to suggest you sent her a note telling her she'd be sorry if she didn't stay away. What can you tell me about that?"

Doctor Patterson moistened his lower lip with his tongue. "Nothing. As I was telling Miss Vale, I know nothing about any note. She made a mistake. One I'm prepared to forgive if you all leave."

"Doctor Patterson has been most unwilling to reveal the truth," I said.

"Because I have nothing else to say," he snapped. "I'm focused on caring for my wife and being a useful part of this community. That is all."

"But not Emily," Patricia said.

Now I had substantial backup, I pressed my luck, moving closer to Patricia and ducking until I was eye level with her. "Tell me why you disliked Emily so intensely?"

"No! I won't have you extracting lies from a sick woman." Doctor Patterson blocked my path. "It'll never hold up in court."

"We're going to court, are we?" I asked.

Doctor Patterson spluttered several words. "Patricia is ill!"

"You're ill," Patricia said. "A bad man. And a thief."

"What's that?" Bishop moved closer, with Jacob by his side. "Has your husband stolen something?"

"No! No! I'm a respected member of this community. Patricia is sick and has terrible memory problems. Leave her be."

"Perhaps you're respected here, but you weren't back in London." Bishop fixed Doctor Patterson with an icy glare. "We'd have been here sooner, but I put in a call to a friend working in a London department. I was aware of the rumours about you, Doctor, so I wanted to see if they were true."

"What rumours are they?" I asked.

"Doctor Patterson didn't move from London because of his wife's failing health," Bishop said. "He was selling his services privately without the appropriate licence."

"That was a misunderstanding." Doctor Patterson's face was bright red again. "I filed the paperwork, but it got lost. It's hardly my fault an administrator was inefficient."

"No paperwork was ever found," Bishop said. "You practised illegally out of a back room in your home for over eighteen months before you were caught."

"I wasn't caught!"

"You were taken to court."

"To pay a fine. Nothing more."

"You were selling prescription medications to whoever could afford them. Often opioids."

Doctor Patterson lifted his chin, an arrogant glint in his eyes. "That was never proven."

"Because of an error on our part," Bishop said with a sigh. "An undercover policeman approached Doctor Patterson to buy prescription medicine. The deal was done, but the evidence was lost. If it hadn't been for that, Doctor Patterson would be behind bars."

"So your wife is right. You are a bad man," I said.

"My wife has barely had a capable thought in her head for years," Doctor Patterson said. "And I only sold medication because it's expensive to care for her. Before I gave up my full-time practice, I had to hire people to watch her, and Patricia hated that. I needed the money for a good reason."

"Did you think you could get away with doing the same thing here?" I asked. "You moved to a seaside town thinking the system would be less sophisticated so you could skim beneath the surface, selling your services and any medications you could get your hands on."

Doctor Patterson glowered at me.

"You must still have your London contacts to provide you with supplies. It would be no trouble to hop on a train and collect them, or perhaps meet halfway. Patricia, does your husband regularly take trips to London?" I asked.

Patricia pursed her lips and squinted as if dredging through her foggy memories. "Half a day every week.

Thursdays. I get lonely on Thursday, even when our neighbour stops by."

"Ignore her! She doesn't know what she's saying." Doctor Patterson continued to glare at me. "And neither do you."

"You have a neighbour who looks in on Patricia when you're out," I said. "It would be simple for us to check to see if you have a regular schedule when you disappear for half a day. What do you think she would tell us?"

Doctor Patterson's face grew even redder. "Our neighbours are our friends. And a man needs respite! I do no harm."

"You do. And that's what Emily found out," I said. "She learned you were supplying drugs to Margate's young people. That's why you're always with them. You're not giving out fatherly advice, you're dispensing illegal medications and recruiting new customers. They visit here on set days because they know you've resupplied."

"You have it all wrong," Doctor Patterson growled out.

"Emily said the same," Patricia said. "But louder and she kept repeating it. My husband was so angry."

"He would be," I said. "And it makes no sense why he needs the extra money, since he's your full-time carer. I suppose he needs to pay his supplier and maybe indulge himself." I looked at Jacob and Bishop, and they both nodded.

"You're coming with me," Bishop said. "I need an official statement and to investigate your whereabouts on the night of Emily's murder."

"I can't leave Patricia!" Doctor Patterson stepped back.

"I could stay with her," I said.

"I'd rather put her in a hospital than leave her with the likes of you," he sneered at me.

"Then your neighbour," I said smoothly.

Doctor Patterson swiped a hand through his hair. "Give me a few moments to sort things out. And before we go anywhere, I'm calling my lawyer."

"You're going to need one," I murmured. We'd got our man.

Chapter 11

"We should order champagne." Ruby raised her hand to alert a waiter about her desire for bubbles. "It's not every day we solve a crime so swiftly and catch such a dreadful rotter."

"I'm not sure champagne is appropriate," I said. "It feels wrong to celebrate with Emily gone."

"Oh! Yes, I suppose you're right. It's hard to know whether to mourn or rejoice." Ruby artfully waved away the waiter. "No champagne. But we won't sit here being glum. We've had a success!"

We were settled around a large dining table in the hotel, having a celebratory dinner. Since we'd caught Doctor Patterson, we all had reason to be cheerful, even though it was tinged with sadness. My mother was there, along with Matthew, Jacob, and Ruby. Bishop had also joined us, and we'd ordered an array of seaside fare, which I was looking forward to eating. Although I'd avoid the fish. I don't think I was made to consume too much seafood.

"Emily was always too busy to attend parties," Bishop said. "She said the pursuit of the truth was the most important thing, and when she was fat, happy, and old, then she'd drink too much champagne and make a fool of herself."

"I wish I'd known her better," Ruby said. "She sounds like just my kind of girl."

"So do I. But justice has been done," I said. "Doctor Patterson's poor alibi, and his wife revealing so much about what he really does when he's supposed to be caring for her, means he won't get away with this crime."

"Although he tried to," Jacob said. "Emily uncovered his tawdry secrets, so he silenced her with a terrifying, watery death. It was a horrible way to go."

"And it was a hateful thing to do," Ruby said. "Doctor Patterson should have come clean. He must know he's in the wrong."

"He claimed he needed the extra money to care for his wife," I said, "but I have my doubts that was his true intent. After all, he had access to her medicines through his work, so he can't have wanted for anything expensive."

"Now he's behind bars, we're looking into his financial records," Bishop said. "Our clean-living doctor has expensive hobbies. Golfing. Trips away. Wine. None of them relate to his wife."

"You should also investigate how much care he really gave Patricia," I said.

"What do you mean?" Bishop asked. "She always appears well cared for."

"I'm no medical expert, but when I spoke to her, she was drowsy and confused. Doctor Patterson refused to tell me what was wrong with her, and no one seems to know what ails Patricia."

Bishop paused and scratched his chin. "I don't believe we've ever discussed her exact illness, just the symptoms."

"It's impolite to pry into a lady's ailments," my mother said.

"What do you think is wrong with her, Veronica?" Ruby asked.

"I believe our shifty doctor has been drugging his wife," I said. "I can't tell you why, but her drowsiness, glassy eyes, and indistinct speech suggest not so much a medical condition but more a drug-induced malady."

"Why would Doctor Patterson drug his own wife?" Bishop asked.

We paused from figuring out that question as our delicious food arrived. Only once the waiters had gone did we recommence.

"Perhaps Patricia discovered what her husband was doing and told him to stop," Jacob said. "He couldn't risk her leaving him or going to the police, so he invented an illness and has been drugging her into silence."

"How long has she been unwell?" I asked Bishop. "Doctor Patterson mentioned she was sick before they moved down from London."

He lifted his gaze to the ceiling as he conducted mental arithmetic. "It wasn't long after they settled here that she became much feebler. Perhaps he upped the dose because she kept trying to escape or get help from the police."

"Doctor Patterson could have promised her he'd changed, but she caught him misbehaving and wouldn't let him get away with it," Ruby said.

I nodded. "And since he looks after her medical needs, no one would question whether the illness was genuine."

"What a terrible man." Ruby sipped her dry martini.

"I need to make a telephone call. This must be looked into. If you'll excuse me." Bishop stood. "Don't wait for me before you start eating. If there's anything behind this theory, we need to help Patricia as soon as possible." He dashed away from the table.

"I can see why you like Bishop," I said to Jacob. "He's effective and efficient. No dallying or making excuses about unnecessary paperwork to complete."

"I get the impression Bishop is enjoying himself. He mentioned to me that he rarely deals with such serious crimes here. He's got used to reprimanding tourists who can't handle their alcohol and misbehaving young people on the beach."

"So a jolly good murder must be thrilling for him," Ruby said. "Although not for poor Emily."

"I wonder how Emily found out about Doctor Patterson's unorthodox behaviour," my mother remarked.

"I have the answer to that," I said. "Mabel gave me a box of Emily's notepads this afternoon when I returned to the Harbour Arms to give her an update, and I've been sifting through them. Her handwriting is appalling, so it's hard to decipher it all. However, Emily made notes about a deceased friend. He died of heart failure, and it was ruled an accident."

"Let me guess, by Doctor Patterson?" Jacob asked.

"One and the same," I said.

Ruby sat forward in her seat. "If Doctor Patterson gave this young man an illegal prescription, and it had an adverse effect, he could be guilty of two murders."

"That's something for the police to investigate," I said. "But Emily was looking into why such a young, fit man dropped down dead. From the notes she made, she was aware he purchased pills from Doctor Patterson before attending a friend's party. The next day, he was dead."

"And fearless Emily confronted Doctor Patterson, demanding answers," Ruby said.

Bishop returned from making his telephone call and settled back in his seat. "I've got some men on the case. We'll interview Patricia and have independent tests taken to see exactly what's in her system. She'll also have a full medical review to see what's wrong with her. If Doctor Patterson has been drugging her, we can add it to his charges."

"Veronica! Tell Bishop about the notepad and the dead friend." Ruby was almost bouncing in her seat with excitement. "With all this bad behaviour we've unearthed about Doctor Patterson, he'll hang for his crimes."

As we ate our delicious food, I got Bishop up to speed with my findings, which caused him to hurry back to the telephone, having barely taken a bite of his meal.

Jacob chuckled. "I remember behaving like that whenever you were around. I thought I'd got on top of things, then you'd unleash a barrage of information, and I'd be investigating all over again."

"That's something I'm sure you don't miss," I said.

His smile wavered for a second, then he nodded. "Not for one second. And I definitely don't miss the paperwork."

Bishop returned again and sighed. Even though he looked tired, there was satisfaction in his eyes. "Doctor Patterson is going nowhere. We're just waiting for him to confess. Unfortunately, he's got an excellent lawyer who is tying us in knots, but we refuse to be deterred. We've got our guilty party. And thanks to Veronica's efforts, it seems we've got him on more than one charge."

"It was nothing," I murmured. "I was happy to assist. Now this matter is cleared up, we can enjoy the rest of our holiday."

"What will happen to Patricia?" Ruby asked. "It could take days for the drugs to get out of her system, so she can't be left alone."

"Patricia has a sister who'll be staying with her," Bishop said. "It's been arranged. They became estranged because she didn't like Doctor Patterson, but when she heard what was going on, she instantly volunteered to help."

"That's excellent news," I said. "Criminal caught and sisters reunited. And we can continue our celebrations tomorrow with a day on the beach. Resting, reading, and eating ice cream. It'll be the proper holiday we promised ourselves."

"With not a murder or a criminal in sight." Ruby raised a glass. "Cheers to that."

Our arrival on the beach the next morning was timed to perfection as the sun came out just as we settled onto the sand. There was even a pleasant breeze, ensuring it wasn't too hot. I'd convinced Matthew and my mother to join us, so the whole family and my friends were there. Benji and Felix bounded around the sand, play-fighting with each other and occasionally dashing towards the waves. It was fun chaos, and I was happy to be in the middle of it.

We'd only been settled for half an hour when Ruby jumped from her towel. "I knew I'd see him! Alfonso can never keep away from the beach. I expect he was hoping he'd find me." She gave me a cheery goodbye wave and dashed over to her new beau.

I watched their passionate kiss before looking away. My gaze settled on Colonel Griffin, who was strolling slowly towards us, dressed in a pale linen suit.

He doffed his hat in greeting. "Splendid day."

"I was just thinking so myself." My mother brightened at his arrival.

"May I encourage you to take a short stroll to the pier?" Colonel Griffin asked her. "We can take our time. The sea breeze is incredibly refreshing."

"I should have the energy for that." My mother sprang up like a teenager and swiftly accepted Colonel Griffin's crooked elbow before they strolled away.

I looked at Matthew. Even though he'd agreed to accompany us to the beach, he wasn't happy. He hid under several large beach towels and appeared to be asleep, just his nose and one closed eye visible. At least he was here. That was progress.

I kept an eye on the dogs while I settled in beside Jacob and closed my eyes. I felt content. The last few months had been terribly stressful with Jacob's accident and his long period of recovery, but things were settling again.

Jacob's warm, solid hand rested on top of mine. "We should visit Mabel later and see how she's doing."

"I telephoned her briefly yesterday evening with the latest," I said. "She was delighted with the arrest but was still puzzled about Doctor Patterson's involvement. Even when I explained everything to her several times, she wasn't convinced."

"Who else could it be? She must still be in shock," Jacob said. "Emily was too young. Her career was just getting started, and it was cut short by a ruthless man who became greedy and didn't have the backbone to confess when caught."

"Doctor Patterson won't be able to harm anybody else ever again," I said.

Jacob's grip tightened on my hand. "I'm warming to having an office here, especially if the cases are this interesting."

"We'll make it work," I said. "This change is good for both of us. It's a new chapter in our lives."

"I like the idea of our lives being combined," Jacob said. "It gives me hope for the future."

"Always have hope. Even in the darkest moments, you'll find a glimmer of it somewhere."

"Good morning." Lady Lizzie Hargreaves's shadow dropped over me as she stopped in front of us. "I hope you don't mind the intrusion, but when I saw you, my curiosity rather got the better of me. It's Miss Vale and Mr Templeton, is it not?"

"Good morning. And you're correct," I said.

She smiled. "Emily told me all about you. I've been intrigued to meet you. You sound fascinating. Lady Elizabeth Hargreave, but everyone calls me Lady Lizzie."

"We saw you at the amusement opening," I said. "What are you curious about?"

"You're working with Inspector Bishop on Emily's murder, aren't you?"

I sat up straighter. "Yes, we've been assisting him."

Lady Lizzie adjusted her large white sun hat and passed her parasol to a waiting assistant. She had three people assisting her. "I had a special interest in Emily and was absolutely shocked to learn what happened to her."

"Emily mentioned you helped with her training," I said.

"I did! She was so excited about becoming a journalist, but it was more than that. She was smart and had a talent for finding a story. When I saw how committed she was to making a name for herself, I wanted to help. I was glad I could do so."

"Emily spoke fondly of you," I said. "She was grateful for your support."

"I always help those with a spark to ignite the future," Lady Lizzie said. "I even invited her to assist with our local literary festival, but she was too busy chasing stories. Good for her, I say."

"I always enjoyed spending time with Emily," I said. "I'm a journalist myself, you see."

"I didn't know that. Intriguing. The things modern women can do today," Lady Lizzie said.

"And you're one of them. From what Emily told me, you're a significant patron of the arts in the area."

"Yes, but only because I come from old family money." Lady Lizzie wrinkled her small nose. "I didn't earn any of it myself. Previous generations were stick-in-the-muds, clinging to the money for fear it would be lost. But what's the point of having it if you don't spend any on worthwhile endeavours? That's what I intend to do. Our family reputation means everything to me. And I encouraged Emily to write about it in the hope it would inspire others to invest in this wonderful town. Sadly, that will no longer be possible."

"I'm sorry she didn't publish your story," I said.

"It is a tragedy," Lady Lizzie said. "The whole business. Is it true our local doctor has been arrested for the crime?"

Jacob stirred into action. "You are well informed."

Lady Lizzie gave a genteel shrug. "It pays to be in the know."

"He is a person of interest," I said.

"How shocking! He attended all of my parties. I shall have to refine my guest list. No killers allowed!"

"How to identify them. That's the tricky part," I said.

Lady Lizzie cocked her head at me. "I'm having another soiree soon to unveil some new building plans. You must both pop by. And your friend there under the towels. He'd be welcome, too. I'm always thrilled to show off my ambitions for Margate. It's a spectacular place, and I intend to ensure the Victorian legacy continues long into the future. With the new train station, opportunities for growth are unlimited."

"We'd be delighted to attend," I said. "We're only here for another week, though."

"Perfect timing. You won't miss a thing. Where are you staying?"

I told her the name of our hotel.

"I'll send an invitation to the front desk, so you have the details. Enjoy the rest of your day." Lady Lizzie strolled off along the sand with her entourage around her.

"How exciting," I murmured. "We have fancy new friends in high places. There are hidden benefits to setting up a base at the seaside."

"Must we go to the party?" Jacob asked.

"I'm sure Lady Lizzie will have the best quality food and champagne," I said. "Doesn't that tempt you?"

"I'd prefer to spend time with you."

My heart warmed. "We'll put in an appearance to be polite."

"I'm not going," Matthew mumbled from under the towels. "Too many people. And I don't enjoy small talk. They probably won't let Felix in, either."

"We'll work something out," I murmured.

We'd only just relaxed back into our deckchairs when Bishop arrived, scattering sand all over Matthew's towels. "There you are! I've been looking for you. I tried the hotel, and they said you'd gone out for the day."

"We deserved a break," I said. "Is something wrong?"

"We have a problem," Bishop said. "Veronica, you were right. Doctor Patterson has been drugging Patricia."

"The very nerve of that man," Jacob said. "What kind of monster drugs his own wife?"

"We'll deal with that matter later," Bishop said. "Now Patricia's head is clearer, she's talking. And what she's telling us puts our prime suspect in the clear. She doesn't think her husband murdered Emily."

Chapter 12

Our relaxing time at the beach was cut sharply short by Bishop's shocking announcement that Patricia believed her husband to be innocent of murder. We dashed back to the hotel to change into more appropriate clothing, as Bishop had arranged for us to visit Patricia in Margate's small cottage hospital, where she'd been admitted the previous evening.

Apparently, after her blood had been taken and examined, the doctors were so alarmed by the amount of substances in her system, they'd decided to monitor her vital signs to ensure she didn't suffer from a shock withdrawal.

"It makes you wonder about who you can really trust." I tugged a suitable dress over my head and smoothed my hair down before glancing at Benji. "You're supposed to be able to trust your husband."

He placed his paw over his nose and wagged his tail.

"I trust you! You adorable fellow."

There was a tap on the door. "Veronica, we need to leave," Jacob said.

"I'll be right with you. Be a good boy," I said to Benji. "You won't be allowed into the hospital, although I'm certain you'd be a great comfort to Patricia. Matthew and Felix will take the best care of you. I'll be back as soon as possible."

He raised one paw again, earning him a scratch behind the ears for being so charming.

Once Benji was safely with Matthew, who'd been delighted to have a reason to return to his room sooner than expected, we were out the door and into Bishop's car, heading towards the cottage hospital, which sat just outside the centre of Margate.

"Does Patricia know she's receiving such a big audience?" Jacob asked.

"She requested Veronica attend," Bishop said. "Although she couldn't remember your name, she described you as the forthright woman who wouldn't back down to her husband. I could only think she meant you."

"That's an apt description," Jacob said with a wry smile.

"I'm proud to be forthright," I said. "How much does Patricia remember?"

"Everything." Bishop had to slow the car as a group of children carrying sticks of rock and candyfloss bundled into the road, joking with each other. "As soon as Doctor Patterson was taken into custody, her regular dosing stopped. He was using a hefty sedative to keep her sleepy, but he couldn't keep her incapacitated at all times. As well as sedatives, the tests revealed muscle relaxants, an opioid derivative, a strong painkiller, and something else we've yet to identify."

Jacob shook his head. "I'd like to ring the doctor's neck."

"There's a long queue to do that," Bishop said. "He's had the wool pulled over all our eyes."

"Including Lady Lizzie," I said. "We met on the beach just before you arrived, and she knew all about Doctor Patterson. She was shocked."

"It's no surprise she has all the relevant information. Lady Lizzie considers Margate to be her town. She once described it as her one true love. And she has an open invitation to our detective chief inspector to dine with her whenever it takes his fancy. She takes him to the best restaurants, so he's always eager to accompany her."

"Lady Lizzie isn't married?" I asked.

"Widowed. And happily so. If you believe the rumours, her husband was a stiff-backed tyrant. He died a few years ago, leaving Lady Lizzie everything, and she's been a free spirit ever since. Rather than hiding in the enormous house her husband left her, she's often seen about town talking to local shop owners about what they'd like to see in Margate. She pays attention to everyone and uses that information to her advantage. My chief always sings her praises. He considers her an excellent woman."

"Your detective chief inspector sounds sweet on her," I said.

"He may be, but I get the impression Lady Lizzie is a thoroughly happy widow with no intention of finding herself a new husband."

"Good for her," I said. "A woman is complete without a man."

Jacob glanced at me, and I leaned over and patted his knee.

"Here we are." Bishop parked outside a small white building, and we headed inside. He spoke to the receptionist, and after a moment, we were led into a private room. It was neat and tidy, with only one bed in it. Patricia was in that bed.

Her eyes were no longer glassy or struggling to focus as they latched onto me. Instead, there was a brilliant anger burning in them. "It's you! You're the one who broke into our home."

"I entered through an open door and announced myself," I said. "I even told you my name. Veronica Vale."

"Veronica! That's it. I thought of so many combinations of names but couldn't get it right. Victoria. Verity. Nothing fit. Here you are. I'm glad of it." She looked at Bishop. "Is there any news about my disgrace of a husband?"

"We're still talking to him," Bishop said.

"The absolute stinker. I veer between anger and tears after having learned exactly what he did to me. Did Inspector Bishop tell you?" She addressed the question to me.

The two men wisely stepped back, sensing Patricia had little interest in dealing with the male sex anytime soon. "Yes. He provided me with a useful summary. What can you remember?"

"I remember my terror. My husband has kept me a prisoner for years! I knew he was up to something, but I didn't realise how devious he was."

"Why did he drug you? Did you learn what he was doing with the illegal prescriptions and confront him?"

"I knew there was something untoward about his actions," Patricia said. "But it was before we even moved to Kent that I had my suspicions. He'd receive visitors late in the evening. I told him I was unhappy about it, but he said he was helping the poor by providing cheap medication. I could hardly complain, but it made me uneasy. And then I grew suspicious when I looked out of an upstairs window and saw a bright and well-dressed young man striding away from the house, pocketing something."

"Is that when you confronted him?" I asked.

"I did. He brushed it off and said I shouldn't worry and focus on keeping our home."

"You never worked?"

"He never let me." Patricia sighed. "I've always wanted a large family. I would have been content if I had several children to look after as well as the home, but it never happened. In truth, I was bored. I wanted to work, but my oh-so sneaky husband informed me that work was a stressor on the body, and we couldn't afford to take that risk. Naturally, I agreed. After all, he was the expert. I've been such an idiot."

"You believed the word of the man you loved and married," I said. "That's not foolish."

"It feels foolish." Patricia's gaze went to the window. "I remained suspicious of him, though, and kept watch. More and more, it was fashionable, well-moneyed types coming to our door. That's when I knew I'd been lied to."

"So you confronted your husband again, and that's when he began drugging you?" I asked.

"He must have done, though I didn't realise it," Patricia said. "I began having headaches, so he prescribed me a powder. When that didn't work, he gave me something else. That's when I became incredibly tired. I was sleeping for hours during the daytime. Not long after that, he decided we were to up sticks and move to Kent. I didn't want to. I have friends and family in London, but I didn't have the strength to argue. Before I knew it, we were here, and I was confined to a chair like an invalid. An invalid he created!"

"Did you ever try to leave?" I asked.

"No! I believed I was genuinely ill. I wasn't desperately unhappy with him, but I was bored stiff. If I'd had the energy, perhaps I would have left, but he drugged me into submission." Patricia thumped her hands on the sheets.

An older woman with curly grey hair entered the room carrying a tray with two cups of tea on it. "Patricia! Are you up to having visitors?"

"I absolutely am. I'm already feeling so much better for having them here." She introduced her sister, Meredith.

Meredith set down the tea tray and folded her arms over her ample bosom. "I knew something was wrong. The moment he said they were leaving London, I got a feeling in my waters. Mother used to get the same feeling, just before disaster struck."

"We call that gut instinct," Bishop said.

"Guts, waterworks, it's all the same to me," Meredith said. "I begged Patricia not to go, but by then she was under his influence."

"Not willingly," Patricia said.

Meredith caught hold of her sister's hand. "He stopped me from visiting. I used to telephone, and when that didn't work, I wrote letters. Patricia never replied to me. Eventually, I got a short note from him saying

Patricia was too sick to write and couldn't be stressed with visitors. I was outraged and upset. I thought she didn't want to see me anymore."

"I'd never do such a terrible thing," Patricia said. "I was desperate for company, but he wouldn't allow it."

"I never liked him," Meredith said. "He was too smug. And he spent all that money on your wedding. There was no need."

"It was extravagant," Patricia murmured, her cheeks flushing. "I wanted a simple wedding, but he spent so much money on a lavish party afterwards."

"As we're discovering, your husband has expensive tastes," Bishop said. "We believe that's the reason he's been selling illegal prescriptions to those who can afford them."

"Where are all these expensive things?" Meredith asked. "Patricia's not seen them. They're hers too."

"We've located a storage unit," Bishop said. "We found cases of wine, golfing equipment, and even a small boat."

Meredith fanned her face. "What a cad. Squandering all that money rather than taking care of his wife. He deserves to rot in prison. And he hurt that young girl, too."

Patricia sighed and shook her head. "As much as I want him to be charged with murder, on the night Emily died, he was home with me."

"Your husband didn't stay at the amusements all evening?" I asked.

"He went out for a short while to see them open. I remember him telling me he wouldn't be long and to look out for the fireworks. He even turned my chair so I could see out of the window clearly and left the curtains open. I fell asleep, but I heard the front door open when he came in. I looked at the time, so I know exactly when he came home. And knowing that Emily died around midnight, he couldn't have done it."

"He's still in trouble though, isn't he?" Meredith asked. "My dreadful brother-in-law won't get away with doing this to Patricia, will he?"

"Doctor Patterson is in serious trouble," Bishop said. "Not just for the illegal prescriptions, but he's associated with a possible death as well."

"Oh my," Patricia said. "What did he do?"

"We can't go into details," Bishop said, "but I assure you, you'll never see him again. Your husband is going away for a very long time."

"That's something," Meredith said with a grunt of satisfaction. "I'll be glad to see the back of him. And just think, Patricia, you'll get to keep all that wine. And the boat! Perhaps you could take up golfing, too."

"I don't want his things. I want a husband who respects me and doesn't ply me with drugs because I won't follow his orders."

"There are good men out there," I said. "They can be a trifle hard to find, but when you find the right one, it'll be worth the wait."

"We're done with all that business," Meredith said. "My husband died in the war, and I can't say I was sad. He was a mean old bugger and free with his fists. We'll rub along fine, just the two of us. Now, about that boat..."

"We'll leave you to it," I said. "I hope you feel better soon, Patricia."

"Thanks to all of you, I'm well on the way to recovery. And thank you so much for saving me from a terrible situation. I would have been stuck in that chair until the day my supposedly loving husband gave me a lethal overdose."

We said our goodbyes and left the cottage hospital. I felt dejected. Everything had fit into place. Emily had called Doctor Patterson out on a lie, confronted him, and he'd pushed her off the pier. The case should be solved. But it was far from it.

Jacob touched my arm. "It was a good effort. The evidence pointed at Doctor Patterson as the guilty party."

"He had an excellent motive for wanting Emily dead," Bishop said. "It's disappointing that we know the truth, but we can't ignore it. Now, I need to go back to the station and deal with our disreputable doctor."

"He'll remain behind bars, won't he?" I asked. "I wouldn't trust him not to do a moonlight flit with everything that's against him."

"Doctor Patterson is going nowhere," Bishop said. "We're investigating his criminal dealings and the death of that young man because of the drugs he sold him."

"That'll be Emily's legacy," I said. "She was the one who unearthed the scandal."

"And I'm happy she did," Bishop said. "Would you like a ride back to the hotel?"

I shook my head. "No, thank you. I could do with a walk. Get some fresh air."

"I'll see you all later." Bishop hurried away.

"Why don't we visit Mabel?" Jacob suggested. "It's better she hears this news from you than some stranger gossiping on a street corner or over a pint of ale."

I didn't want to break the bad news, but Jacob was right. Mabel deserved to know what was going on. Just as we thought we'd put this mystery to bed, it rolled out, did a large stretch, and decided to have a jolly good day out.

A half-hour walk brought us to the Harbour Arms. The pub was yet to open, but Mabel was there when we knocked on the door. She welcomed us inside.

"I know I should feel happy this is over, but none of it brings Emily back." She led us to a table by the window so we could take in the sea view.

"About that, I have bad news," I said. "Did Bishop tell you about Patricia?"

"He did! I almost fell off my chair when I heard what's been going on," Mabel said. "She hasn't passed, has she? That would be a terrible tragedy."

"Patricia is recovering well," I said. "She's also got her memories back. And unfortunately, she remembers her husband being with her at the time of Emily's murder. He couldn't have killed her."

Mabel sat back in her seat, her eyes wide. "But Emily was investigating his bad behaviour. That was his motive for killing her. At first, I wasn't convinced it was him, but when you told me everything, I had to accept it."

"Doctor Patterson seemed like the perfect suspect," Jacob said. "And he had every reason to silence Emily, but it wasn't him."

"The police aren't letting him go, though, are they?" Mabel asked.

"No, he has a number of serious offences to answer for," I said. "Doctor Patterson is guilty, but not of murdering Emily."

Mabel was quiet for a moment, fiddling with a bar mat as she looked out the window at the beautiful view I was certain she wasn't taking in. "Where does that leave us?"

"We should return to Tommy McAllister," I said. "I'm unsure if Bishop dug up anything about him or his alibi."

"Tommy? Maybe it was him." Mabel pursed her lips. "Although I think the cad act is just that, because it keeps trouble from his door. If people are scared of you, they don't come after you."

"Who else could it be?" I asked.

"Wait here a moment. I found a final box of Emily's notepads. I missed it at first, because it was tucked right under her bed in the middle. There's something in there that may give you a new suspect."

Anticipation fluttered through me as we waited for Mabel to return.

"Who could it be?" Jacob asked. "Surely, Emily wouldn't have made so many enemies in her short life."

"It's surprising how unpopular you can be when you're a journalist," I said. "People don't enjoy their secrets being dug into and exposed to the world."

"I can well understand that," Jacob said.

Mabel returned and placed a notebook in front of me. "Emily was investigating our local councillor, George Havisham."

"What's he been up to that piqued Emily's interest?" I flicked open the notepad.

"I can't say for certain, but Emily wrote to him asking for details about fishing permits," Mabel said.

"Why would that be an issue?" Jacob asked. "This is a seaside town, and I've seen the trawlers going in and out."

"I couldn't tell you," Mabel said, "but in Emily's notes, she details that she wrote to him on six separate occasions and was ignored. She also telephoned a dozen times and even visited his office. After her last visit, she wrote that he sent her back a short note suggesting she mind her own business."

"The business being the distribution of permits to fish?" I asked.

"I believe so. I don't know if it's useful," Mabel said, "but there's something odd about it."

"Odd indeed." I took a moment to decipher Emily's scrawling handwriting. "If your local councillor is hiding a fishy secret, we need to find out what it is."

Chapter 13

I set down the telephone in the hotel lobby and turned to Jacob. "Councillor Havisham is all in favour of new businesses setting up in Margate. He's happy to meet this afternoon to talk over the plans for our private investigation firm."

"That was fast work. Local council members in London are slow to respond to any meeting requests. Even from the police." Jacob winced as we walked away from the reception desk.

"I can be very persuasive. Now, it's time for you to rest," I said. "Your leg is troubling you."

"No more than usual."

"Our quiet morning on the beach lasted less than an hour," I said. "A big part of this trip to the seaside was to ensure your successful recovery, and I've been remiss in focusing on that." I made a show of taking his arm, but secretly it was to give Jacob support as the pained expression remained on his face.

"I've had plenty of rest. And I like to be active. It's what I'm used to."

"And I like you to be healthy. You'll need to be fit to run an effective agency. I can't have my staff constantly going off sick."

"I'm your staff now?" He arched an eyebrow. "We're not equal partners in this venture?"

"It's something for us to discuss." I picked a piece of lint off his sleeve. "We're not meeting Councillor Havisham until four pm. That'll give us time to rest and enjoy a leisurely lunch. And I must catch up with my mother and Matthew."

"And Ruby," Jacob said.

"We know where she'll be. We'll be lucky if we can drag her back to London at this rate." I paused by the entrance to a small orangery, a room full of glass, light, and fragrant plants. My mother reclined in the shade on a comfortable sofa.

"I'll leave you to it, shall I?" Jacob asked.

"If by leaving me to it, you mean you'll go straight to your room and rest that leg, then yes," I said. "And arrange for room service. We'll dine together properly this evening."

He sighed and grumbled for a few seconds, but Jacob's lack of serious protest revealed how much his leg troubled him. "Very well. But don't sneak off and meet the councillor without me."

"I wouldn't dream of such a thing." I deliberately didn't watch him walk away, because I knew he'd be limping, and he'd hate to see me notice. Instead, I headed into the orangery. My mother appeared to be asleep, her feet up and her eyes closed.

"It looks like you've had a busy morning." I settled on the edge of the sofa.

She opened her eyes. "I think I'll need another holiday after this one."

"Has Colonel Griffin worn you out by being so charming and thoughtful?"

My mother pursed her lips. "He appreciates that I'm not well and is most considerate of my needs."

"As he should be. He's a kind man. An excellent dresser, too. Did I notice a pocket watch? You don't see many of those around these days."

"Don't go getting ideas in that head of yours," my mother said sharply. "We're simply of a similar age and have plenty of topics of conversation we enjoy debating."

"What idea do you think I have?"

"Romantic notions. I won't have it. I leave that sort of thing to you and Ruby."

I didn't press my mother. Her heart had been savagely broken when my father died, and I'd feared she'd never recover. And in truth, she never fully did. Her heart palpitations and aches were down to her tragic loss. We all grieve differently, and hers comes out in physical pains. Whereas mine resulted in a steely focus on work, doing good, and never pausing long enough to recall the tragedy that surrounded my father's death.

"Is Ruby not with you?" my mother asked.

"Don't you remember? She dashed off after her Italian friend."

"I admire you young ones, pursuing romance, but you must tell her to be careful," my mother said. "She could get herself a reputation."

"I'm keeping an eye on things, but I'm hopeful this is just a holiday romance."

My mother huffed out a breath. "Well, good for her, I suppose. And if she does make an embarrassment of herself, it's not as if she lives here. We'll be back in London before we know it. What about Jacob?"

"I sent him up to his room. His leg was troubling him, even though he wouldn't admit it."

"It's good he's got you looking after him. And I'm happy you're finally together."

"Let's not jump to conclusions," I said. "We're not together. We're puzzling through things. And there's no rush."

My mother sat up a little straighter. "No rush! After he almost died, you should rush. You never know what's around the corner. Losing your father showed us that. And as for the Great War, who could have predicted so many years of uncertainty and fear?"

"There had been rumblings of unrest in governments for a long time," I said, "but I see your point. I intend to take things slowly, though. If we rush, we could make a mistake."

"And if you don't rush, you could miss an opportunity of a lifetime," my mother said. "Don't you want a whirlwind romance? Someone who makes your heart race and your cheeks flush with joy?"

"That sounds dreadfully messy," I said. "How is Matthew?"

"Sliding downhill too quickly for my liking. He wouldn't talk to me after we got back from the beach. He keeps shaking, too. Do you remember the tremors he had when he first came home?"

I nodded. Matthew had barely been able to speak or attend to any of his personal needs when he arrived back from serving his country. There had been talk of having him put in an asylum because the doctor thought he'd lost his senses. My mother and I put our foot down about that and were determined to keep him at home.

"This break has been rather less relaxing than I'd anticipated," I said.

"Murder does that to a person. What news about Emily?" my mother asked. "You dashed off the beach before I had an opportunity to ask. Has a new clue surfaced?"

"A problem and a clue," I said. "Patricia, Doctor Patterson's wife, revealed he was with her at the time Emily died. I was so certain he'd done it."

"Surely, she was under the influence of medication, so she can't be relied upon," my mother said.

"Patricia was coherent when I met with her," I said. "She even remembered the time her husband returned home from the new amusements. As much as I wanted it to be him, it isn't."

"What new clue did you find? Have you uncovered a roguish fellow who did Emily wrong?" Although my mother pretended to be appalled by my dabbling in murder investigations, the scandal secretly thrilled her.

"In a manner of speaking," I said. "We stopped by the Harbour Arms after visiting Patricia at the hospital and learned that Mabel has uncovered more information from Emily's notebooks. Apparently, she'd been investigating a local councillor, George Havisham. Something to do with fishing licences."

"I can't see how that could be connected to what happened to Emily. Has Mabel made a mistake?"

"I'm perplexed, too. But it seems Emily was onto something, because Councillor Havisham refused to meet her," I said. "I've arranged a meeting with him this afternoon with Jacob on the pretence of discussing our new office in Margate."

My mother sighed. "You're still determined to go through with that?"

"It's a perfect solution. Jacob has warmed to the idea, and he's seen what opportunities Margate holds. It's a thriving town, and as the population grows, so will the complexity of the cases. The local police do what they can, but an experienced private investigator on hand to assist will be welcome. Especially since Jacob already has connections here."

"If you have an office in Margate to look after, I won't see so much of you," my mother said. "Who will take care of me?"

"As well you know, you're capable of looking after yourself," I said. "You choose not to. That's the difference."

"I don't make my own feet ache and my heart race," my mother protested.

I took hold of one of her hands and gently pressed it between mine. "Is that true? You fret and worry about everything. That's unhealthy. And I know how much you miss Daddy. You rarely talk about him, but I can see it in your eyes."

She gripped my hand. "I do miss him. And I'm angry with him. I never thought he'd leave us. Especially not like that."

"He had a hectic life. Maybe we missed a sign something was wrong. I was so busy forging my path at the London Times, and I neglected him. I should have spent more time with him."

"There's no use you thinking that, or you'll end up in a sickbed like me," my mother said.

I arched an eyebrow. "Is that you admitting some of your maladies are self-induced?"

"Foolish child! You can't make yourself ill by thinking about it."

I was certain that wasn't true, but that was a debate for another time. Holding in grief and not expressing concerns took a toll on a person's health. If you had no outlet for your worries and no conduit to filter your grief through, you buried it inside, and it festered. I was guilty of doing the same thing, but I still talked about my father. Talking may not cure all problems, but it eased the burden.

My mother's gaze shifted to the window. "He'd be happy we were here. Your father loved visiting the seaside."

I smiled as a happy memory played through my mind of me as a child, on the beach with Matthew as my parents sat in deckchairs. "He wanted more pubs in this county. It'll be good for me to have a base here, because I can keep an eye on things more easily. And I must make sure Jacob has a useful purpose. Losing his job with the police almost broke him."

"You're always thinking of others," my mother said. "But perhaps you're right. So long as you don't come down here all the time. And there'll be no talk of you moving out. Your home is with me."

"As if I'd trust you and Matthew on your own," I said. "Have no fears. I'm remaining with you. But regular weekends in Kent overseeing our pubs and getting to know Jacob is a positive thing. After all, you keep insisting he's the perfect man for me."

"Perhaps he's not so perfect if he takes you down here and away from me."

"It's a train ride away," I said. "And now you've discovered that being out of your sickbed can be enjoyable, you may like to do it more often. Perhaps even to visit your new friend, Colonel Griffin."

"I'll think about it," my mother said. "But there won't be any more trips for some time. It'll take me at least two months to recover from this one."

Lady Lizzie appeared in the orangery, a vision in cream silk and feathers. "We must stop bumping into each other like this."

"It is becoming a habit," I said to her. "Have you been introduced to my mother? Edith Vale."

"A pleasure," Lady Lizzie said. "I'm having a luncheon party here. The hotel does excellent food. Did you know, the chef is from France? He came over during the war and settled, declaring Margate to be magnificent. And I couldn't agree more."

"We've enjoyed plenty of delicious meals while staying here," my mother said.

Lady Lizzie hesitated then edged closer. "I hope you don't think me too nosy, but I heard a whisper that Doctor Patterson isn't to be charged with Emily's murder. Since you're in the thick of it, I wanted to know if it was true."

"You do work fast in gathering the gossip," I said. "Where did you get that information?"

"I have friends in high places," Lady Lizzie said with a light laugh. "In truth, the police commissioner's wife telephoned me. Apparently, the men have been gossiping about the investigation, and she heard a few snippets. Is it true? He's innocent?"

"Well, I shouldn't tell you, but you'll know soon enough." I checked no one was within hearing range. "Doctor Patterson is to be charged with some serious offences, but not Emily's murder."

"That's a turn-up for the books." Lady Lizzie paused to wave at her guests as they passed the orangery. "I was surprised when the police considered him guilty. He's done so much good for this town."

"When you hear more rumours about him, you may change your mind," I said.

Lady Lizzie stepped closer, her eyes alight with interest. "Would you care to share? I'll be the envy of my friends if I obtain the latest gossip first."

"I shouldn't say more," I said. "But Doctor Patterson won't be a free man for a very long time."

"How scandalous!" Lady Lizzie clutched her pearls. "I must visit his poor wife. She's in the hospital, isn't she?"

"Yes, and recovering well," I said. "We learned Doctor Patterson's care wasn't as tender and loving as it should have been."

"Oh, my." Lady Lizzie pressed a hand against her chest. "There was I, thinking I was the queen of information gathering, but you've outshone me by a country mile."

"We've yet to solve what happened to Emily, though," I said. "So if you hear more whispers or rumours, please let me know."

Lady Lizzie took a step back. "I'd be happy to. I really should see to my guests, but..."

"You have whispers to share?" I asked.

"I don't like to tattle, but I will tell you one thing that's been troubling me."

"What's that?" I said at the same time as my mother.

"Emily mentioned a problem with one of Tommy's girls. Do you know them? The flamboyant types who perform at his club. The ones with the stage makeup and tiny outfits. I like to think I'm modern minded, but that stretches my boundaries of acceptability."

"I know who you mean." I decided not to mention that we'd been to a club and spoken to one of those ladies.

"Apparently, there was an argument between Emily and a dancer. I'm not sure what it was about, but those ladies are street-smart and one may dare to say—dangerous. They know what they want and do whatever they must to get it."

"Even murder?" My mother's eyes were wide with excitement.

"I can't say for certain. It may only be rumours."

"Do you know the name of the dancer Emily argued with?" I asked.

"The bold one, with short blonde hair. Iris? Or it could be Ivy."

I disguised my surprise. Ivy Vance helped Bishop with his investigations. Was that why she was being so helpful? Had she done something to Emily and wanted to ensure the police weren't onto her?

"Anyway, it's been delightful to see you, but I must go," Lady Lizzie said. "Enjoy the rest of your day." She swept out of the orangery, leaving a muddle of thoughts and questions in my head.

"What do you think about that?" my mother asked.

"I think I need a word with Ivy to see what she's been concealing from us."

Chapter 14

I rolled onto my side and used my hands to cushion my head. After a light lunch of sandwiches and a pot of tea, I'd followed my own advice and headed to my room for a restorative nap. Before settling in, I'd lightly tapped on Jacob's door, but when he didn't answer, I assumed he was already asleep. It would do him good. And I'd keep an eye on him to ensure he kept taking his pain medication. Men were such horrors at not following sensible advice when it came to their health.

Although I'd napped, I'd kept stirring as I'd considered Lady Lizzie's words about Ivy and her possible involvement in what happened to Emily. What had they fought about? Ivy had clearly known Emily, but how close were they? Ivy said she'd attended a private party after working at the club. If she'd been there, she couldn't have been on the pier, pushing Emily over the side.

I checked the time. We had half an hour until we were meeting Councillor Havisham. I stood, tidied my clothing, and freshened up in the bathroom.

Benji rolled off the bed and did an enormous stretch.

"Are you ready for some bracing sea air?" I asked him. "For once, you won't have to stay behind. You're such a good boy, putting up with me coming and going. I promise, when we have the office here, we'll make it dog-friendly. We'll put a fresh bowl of water outside every morning, and there'll be a tin of biscuits freely available for passing dogs. I'll make that a condition of Jacob's employment."

Benji wagged his tail as if he considered those to be excellent ideas.

We left the room, and I knocked on Jacob's door. He opened it a few seconds later, looking refreshed after his sleep.

"We're ready to go when you are," I said.

"I'll be right with you. Come in."

I stepped inside his room. He kept the place tidy, and I was happy to note his pain medication bottle on the table beside the bed. "Are you up to date with your pills?"

He glanced at me as he shrugged on his jacket. "I took them before I went to sleep, so they'll hold me over for at least two more hours." He picked up a folder and tucked it under his arm.

"Good idea. We need to make sure we look serious about our business," I said.

"We are serious." Jacob collected his room key and followed me out before locking the door and giving Benji a swift pat. "The folder doesn't have details of our private investigation firm, though."

"Oh! Are you planning on showing Councillor Havisham the other office details?" We'd arranged to meet outside our preferred office to get his thoughts on the location. While we might be grilling him about his involvement with Emily, he was a local man and would have useful information that could sway us one way or the other regarding where to take premises.

"No. It's not that. And if you're happy, I'd like us to take the lease on the last office we looked at." Jacob walked beside me and Benji along the corridor and down the stairs. "It's ideal and will serve us well for several years. We may want to expand at a later date, but this gives us room to grow and is a manageable price."

"I like your thinking," I said. "Ambitious already. Very well, if that's the one for you, then we shall take it. We can have another peek around the outside after we've finished speaking with Councillor Havisham to make sure it's structurally sound."

"It looked fine to me," Jacob said. "But it's good to be thorough."

I glanced at the folder again. "So, if you don't have details about the other offices with you, what's in there?"

"Something I've been trying to talk to you about ever since this holiday began," Jacob said. "It's important."

"But it's not about our business?" I slowed and turned to him. "If you're having second thoughts, tell me now. I don't want us to sign the lease and then you reveal it was a big mistake."

"No! It's a solid idea. I've even talked it over with Bishop, and he said the police don't have the specialist skills to tackle serious crime. Bishop is the most experienced of all of them, and he's the only one. Although there is talk of getting more training. That takes time."

"Then there's nothing to discuss. Provided the police will work with you during your investigations, I see no problem." I left a note at the reception desk to let my mother, Ruby, and Matthew know we were going out, then we headed into a cool but pleasant late afternoon. There was a hazy sun in the sky and the sharp tang of sea salt in the air, mingling with the smell of freshly cooked chips.

"Provided we can establish regular visits, you down here and me up to London, I see no problems, either," Jacob said.

"The train will make that very possible." I was still wary of what was in the folder. "Ruby has grown charmed by Margate, so she can sometimes bring us down in her car."

"I'd prefer it if you used the train," Jacob said. "Ruby doesn't know the meaning of the word brake pedal."

I chuckled. "She can be speedy. She enjoys the racing line."

"Then she should become a race driver, not scare you half to death every time you sit in the passenger seat of her Ghost," Jacob said.

Still curious as to what was in Jacob's folder, I asked, "This talk you want to have, it's not about my mother, is it?"

"Why would it be about her?"

"Has she been pestering you to make an honest woman out of me?"

"No! But it is serious."

I sighed, a small breath of frustration. "I can tell. Very well, if we must, we'll talk about it. But not now. I need to focus on Councillor Havisham and see what he's hiding about his fishing licences."

"And why Emily was so interested in them," Jacob said.

Councillor Havisham was five minutes late for our appointment, so we had ample opportunity to walk around the building we were considering leasing. The foundations and walls seemed sound, as did the roof. It was another positive sign we were doing the right thing.

"My apologies, dear lady. I was about to leave my desk when I received an urgent telephone call. Please forgive me for making you wait." Councillor Havisham extended a hand for me to shake, but the second he saw Jacob, he changed direction and offered it to him first.

"The weather is pleasant enough to be standing outside," I said. "We appreciate you meeting us at such short notice."

"It is my honour, and it's also my duty." Councillor Havisham's voice had a weedy warble to it. "I serve the local community. And if you're considering investing in our marvellous town, you'll become a local resident too, and therefore, I am your humble servant." He looked at Jacob, nodding vigorously. "So, this is the building you're considering, is it?"

"Yes, it's an ideal location." I was determined to lead this conversation. Councillor Havisham was obviously an old-fashioned sort who preferred to speak only to men on matters of business, but we were past that fuddy-duddy nonsense.

"It's an excellent spot," Councillor Havisham said. "A ten-minute walk to the seafront and all the amusements, good foot traffic, and on a regular bus route. The new train station is barely fifteen minutes from here. You have all the conveniences on your doorstep."

"And the rent is reasonable," Jacob said. "We'd like to start with a three-year lease to see if this is the kind of business Margate wants."

"I'm sure we can iron out the fine details with the right deal in place." Councillor Havisham rubbed his hands together. "I must admit, when your dear wife told me of your plans over the telephone, I was surprised. But I thought about it, and we have been having trouble with our police. They're capable chaps on the whole, but as Margate expands and becomes even more glorious, life can become a touch more complicated, if you get my meaning."

"I'm glad you mentioned that," I said, deciding not to correct him over our marital status. "We're aware of a young woman who recently died. She was pushed off the pier."

Councillor Havisham blinked owlishly, and a faint flush crept up his neck and onto his cheeks. "Don't worry yourself about that. The police believe it was an accident. Some of these young people get foolish when they've had too much to drink."

"That's true, but I knew Emily," I said. "I own the Harbour Arms and am well acquainted with Mabel, my landlady."

"You own a pub?" Councillor Havisham's tone didn't hide his disbelief. "That's hardly a fitting profession for a lady of your calibre."

"I'm charmed you can discern my calibre from such a brief encounter," I said. "The business passed to me after my father died."

"Oh! I should have recognised the surname. I met your father at the Harbour Arms several times. An excellent fellow. I heard he passed. You have my deepest sympathy."

"Thank you. He always wanted me to run the business alongside him. I've been getting familiar with how things work alongside my own job."

"Two jobs! What is the world coming to when a woman needs two jobs to sustain herself?" Councillor Havisham glanced at Jacob. "Do you not support your wife, sir?"

I gently cleared my throat. "We're going into business as partners but not as husband and wife."

"Well! I ... I see. I sometimes get called a little behind the times, and I guess this is one of those occasions," Councillor Havisham said. "Goodness me. You've rather taken me aback."

"That won't be a problem, will it?" Jacob asked.

"No. Absolutely not. It's just unusual." Councillor Havisham appeared at a loss for words.

I steered the conversation to a relevant topic. "Of course, if serious crime in Margate continues to rise, perhaps it'll be too dangerous to set up a business." I attempted to sound demure, but I wasn't sure it worked.

That got his attention. "What happened to young Emily was a tragedy, but an isolated incident. And the police are on the case. I imagine they'll wrap things up in a day or two. Margate is the best town in this county. I want to ensure it retains its Victorian vigour. A safe place for people who live here and a tourist destination for all."

"We look forward to having a base here," Jacob said.

"And I shall be certain to visit you when you do," Councillor Havisham said. "Perhaps we can have one of those official ribbon-cutting ceremonies. They seem to be all the rage these days, don't they?"

"We attended the opening of the amusements where Lady Lizzie cut a ribbon," I said. "That was the night Emily died. Did you know her?"

Councillor Havisham tugged at a shirt cuff. "No, but I was aware of her. I believe she was training to be a journalist."

"That's right. In fact, she wrote to you on numerous occasions about concerns she had over fishing licences."

He cocked his head, a flash of surprise crossing his face. "I can't say I recall any correspondence. If Emily wanted a fishing licence, I'm not the man to speak to. I have administrators who deal with the paperwork."

"You don't work with the local fishermen?" Jacob asked.

"Yes, absolutely. It's a special interest. I lead in areas of commerce and business development. That was why I was so thrilled to get your telephone call about opening an office in the area."

"What if Emily didn't want a fishing licence," I said, "but she wanted to talk to you about your work with the fishing trawlers that use Margate as a base? Would that have been something you could have helped with?"

"I would, but we never met." Councillor Havisham fidgeted with his tie.

"Emily wrote to you, attempted to visit your office, and in her notes, she said you replied, telling her to keep her nose out of things that didn't concern her."

Councillor Havisham grew even more flustered. "I'd never do anything of the sort. This is a misunderstanding. Even if Emily wrote to me, my secretary deals with my correspondence. And I get a lot. This is my third term serving this town, and I'm proud to be such a popular councillor."

"You really have no recollection of Emily attempting to reach you?" I asked. "When she set her mind to something, she was persistent."

"I'm sorry, I can't help," Councillor Havisham said. "My secretary is diligent. Any trivial matters that come my way, she passes to the appropriate department. I focus on the exciting business development and the big plans we have for Margate. To make it a glorious town."

"Did you attend the opening of the new amusements?" I asked.

"Alas, I missed that fun. I usually go to those sorts of things, but Lady Lizzie is more involved in the private development. I handle the public money while she invests her funds for the good of the town. We have a solid working relationship."

"Even though she's a woman?" I couldn't resist a small dig.

Councillor Havisham flushed again as Jacob shot me a filthy look. "Lady Lizzie and her family go back generations in Margate. She's a wonderful patron of the arts. We couldn't desire a more benevolent benefactor. It was a pity I missed her opening the amusements, but I had a late council meeting."

"How late?" I asked.

"These things drag on for hours. Some people like to hear the sound of their own voice," Councillor Havisham said.

I could well believe he was one of them. "What did you do after the meeting ended?"

He hesitated. "Why do you want to know?"

"Veronica is fascinated by local politics. She's considering getting involved." Jacob smoothed my bluntness.

"Oh, my dear lady, you have enough going on without considering the complicated world of politics. After my meeting, I went home to bed. It's exhausting, keeping the town thriving." He checked the time. "If you'll excuse me, I really must go. Best of luck with your new venture."

"Thank you for your time," Jacob said as Councillor Havisham dashed off with barely a goodbye. "Veronica! You chased him away."

"There was no chasing!"

"You made him nervous with all your questions."

"Councillor Havisham was already nervous as soon as we started talking about Emily," I said. "Could he really have been at a council meeting until midnight?"

"He was most likely at home asleep in bed with his wife by that time."

"That's an alibi we must check," I said. "And I don't believe him about not knowing Emily wanted to meet with him. He was hiding something."

Jacob drew in a deep breath. "I know you don't like advice, but I'm giving you some. Sometimes, charging in with blunt questions creates a wall of silence. Tact and diplomacy go a long way, especially with public figures like Councillor Havisham. He's a man who expects to be respected, not grilled like a criminal."

"Perhaps he is a criminal." I sighed. "But I should have taken a step back. I suspect you'd have got more out of him if I hadn't been here. He's definitely a man's man."

"I don't disagree." Jacob turned towards the sea. "Let me handle the councillor. I'll ask Bishop and see if we can dig up anything on him."

"I have no objections to that," I said. "And now we've spoken to him, we need to consider Ivy as a suspect."

"Ivy Vance! We already have plenty of suspects."

"Lady Lizzie told me about Ivy and Emily having a disagreement, so we can't discount her."

"We'll discuss Ivy later." Jacob pulled the folder out from under his arm. "Now—"

"Oh my! What a stroke of luck I found you here." Ruby rushed over, looking flustered and happy.

"I've missed you today," I said. "Don't tell me you've been with your Italian friend all this time?"

She bounced on her toes. "I have. And I have the most thrilling news. We're getting married."

Chapter 15

I stared at Ruby as she stood in front of me, the giant smile on her face and the gleam in her eyes suggesting this marriage announcement wasn't a joke. "Could you repeat that?"

She laughed girlishly. "You silly old thing. There's no need to look so shocked. It had to happen one day."

"Who are you marrying?" Jacob asked.

"There is only one man who has stolen my heart," Ruby said.

"Is it the duke your brother introduced you to?" I asked. "The one with the castle in Scotland? You said you loved him."

"Oh! No! Not him. He was dull."

"The restaurant owner who promised you dessert for breakfast every day? That prospect had you swooning."

Ruby swatted my arm, still smiling. "Stop teasing. I was never serious about him. My waistline would have been ruined!"

"Then I don't know who we are talking about," I said.

"Alfonso! My new Italian friend. Well, he's now much more than a friend." Ruby extended her left hand. There was no ring on her finger. "He's looking at rings as I speak."

"It was a spur-of-the-moment proposal?" Jacob asked.

Ruby grinned. "Yes! He wanted to wait, but he couldn't hold back. Isn't that romantic?"

I opened my mouth, but no suitable words came out. I closed it and continued to stare at my friend. Had she taken leave of her senses? Perhaps she had sunstroke.

"I was as stunned as you when he got down on one knee on the pier and proposed," Ruby said. "He even shed a little tear. Alfonso is hopelessly devoted to me. He told me he loved me during our second day together."

"That's ... unusual." Jacob kept glancing at me, but I had yet to form a coherent thought. In fact, there was a loud buzzing in my ears, and stars sparkled in my vision. Maybe I was the one with sunstroke and this was a terrible hallucination.

"Unusual, but so sweet," Ruby said. "The heart knows when something is meant to be."

"You've stopped breathing," Jacob whispered into my ear.

I gasped in a breath. "What exactly has your heart told you?"

"That I've found true love," Ruby said. "Oh, Veronica, Alfonso is smashing, and so different from all the other men I've fancied. He has an exciting career. He's an experienced traveller. He's seen the world and is knowledgeable about more than the latest fashion from Savile Row or who's who at a particular party. He's a breath of fresh air, and I can't get enough of him."

"Congratulations," Jacob said cautiously. "This holiday is turning into quite an adventure for all of us, don't you think, Veronica?"

"I think ... I think I need a moment." I turned and strode away, paying no attention to the direction I walked. Benji hurried along beside me, his tail and ears down, sensing trouble.

"Veronica, wait! Aren't you going to congratulate me, too?" Ruby hadn't taken my hint and pursued me with purposeful vigour.

"Why did he propose?" I was speaking before I turned towards her. "What did you tell Alfonso to make him so keen on you?"

"Tell him? You're making no sense. He proposed because he loves me and wants to spend the rest of his life with me. Isn't that why most men propose to a woman?"

"Sometimes it is, but sometimes they propose because they want something."

"Oh! You're talking about romance. I have everything under control in that department." A faint blush crossed Ruby's cheeks.

"I find that highly unlikely," I said. "When you're thinking with your heart, you act illogically."

"Love has a certain delightful chaos to it," Ruby said, not deterred by my sharpness. "You know I always like a little chaos."

I wanted to grab her and shake her but settled for digging my fingernails into my clenched hands. "How much does Alfonso know about your family?"

"I've told him everything. We have no secrets."

"He knows they're not wealthy?"

Ruby's brow furrowed. "What does that have to do with anything?"

Jacob approached, but I gestured for him to keep back. I had to get to the bottom of why a stranger had proposed to my best friend. "Ruby, think carefully. What exactly did you tell Alfonso about your situation?"

"He ... he knows I work for Lady M. And I love horses. I told him about my brothers and sister."

"And your parents? What did you say they did for work?"

"I told him the truth. They're entrepreneurs."

"And how successful did you say they were in their entrepreneurial endeavours?"

A notch formed between Ruby's eyebrows. "I really don't know what this has to do with me finally finding a delightful man to marry. A man I actually want to marry."

I gently massaged my forehead with the tips of my fingers. "You can't fall in love in a few days."

"Some of us do. Some of us aren't focused on logic and practicalities and not wanting to make things messy. Love is a whirlwind of joy."

I glanced at Jacob, who was within earshot but pretending not to hear. "I trust you're planning a long engagement so you can get to know each other thoroughly. In this day and age, it's a simple enough matter to break off an engagement if you change your mind."

Ruby's happy demeanour shifted as she folded her arms across her chest. "We don't want to wait. We've already looked into it, and there's a charming registry office in Margate. If we complete the paperwork now, we can be married on the last day of our holiday. It'll be the perfect end to our getaway. And now Emily's murder is solved, you'll have plenty of time to help me find a dress, food, and flowers. There's so much to do."

"The end of the holiday? But that's barely any time. I won't allow it," I said.

"Veronica! As much as I value your friendship, you have no say in whether I marry. It's my decision, and I said yes. Why can't you be happy for me?"

I couldn't hold back my anger. "Because you're blundering into a horrible mistake. You've been so focused on this Italian stranger, you don't even know Emily's killer is still on the loose. Maybe it's your new fiancé."

Ruby jerked back. "Oh! That's a silly thing to say. He's an angel."

"Have you asked Alfonso if he has a criminal record?"

"Of course not!"

"You should." I was letting my fury fill my words with venom, but how outlandish was the suggestion Ruby marry this person?

"I will forgive those words because you've had a surprise, and I know you don't like surprises," Ruby said stiffly. "And I didn't know about the blip in the investigation. I thought the police had charged Doctor Patterson with Emily's murder."

"He's guilty of plenty of things, but not of ending Emily's life," I said. "And I have no time to indulge in your wedding fantasies. We've just been talking to another suspect, Councillor Havisham. And Ivy Vance, the dancing girl we met, is also a suspect."

"Goodness, I have missed a lot," Ruby said. "But I have the perfect excuse. I've been so enchanted by my new beau."

"Bewitched by his lies," I said. "I never trust a man who's too charming. It usually hides a deficit of character."

Ruby wrinkled her nose. "Well, you have no concerns about being too charmed by Jacob. I've never seen him make a romantic gesture in his life. Unless you count feeding Benji treats."

Actually, I did. Kindness to animals was a top-quality character trait. "Leave Jacob out of this."

Ruby scowled at me. "I always knew you were a prickly type, but I never put you down as a man-hater. Although, the way you've kept Jacob on a long lead for such a long time, I should have known the truth."

"A long lead! How dare you. Jacob has always been clear as to my intentions." I glanced at him, daring him to contradict me.

Wisely, his gaze was fixed on the sea, and he still pretended he couldn't hear every word we were saying.

I pointed a finger at Ruby. "And just because one takes time to assess a situation and ensure it's suitable doesn't mean they're wasting anybody else's time."

"And just because one jumps in bravely with both feet when something feels right doesn't mean it's wrong," Ruby said. "Why be so stubborn about this? Our opposite natures have always clicked. That's why we're such good friends. I wanted your happiness. Instead, I get this."

I pressed my lips together, forcing back an angry retort. We'd been the firmest of friends for such a long time, and I refused to let a man put a wedge between us. Especially a stranger who I'd yet to meet properly but was already suspicious of.

Ruby stepped forward, a conciliatory look on her face. "I am sorry for being so distracted. You knew Emily and liked her, and I should have paid more attention and helped in the investigation."

"There's no apology needed. Even if you were involved, I'm not sure we'd be any farther along. It appears Emily put a lot of noses out of joint, and we've yet to discover which one she bent out of shape the most."

"A dancer and a councillor, you say? I really am out of the loop. Love makes you ditzy," Ruby said.

"And mildly insane," I muttered.

"What do you mean by that?"

"Ruby, come to your senses," I said. "Marrying a stranger is outrageous. You can't know a person in a few days. We always put on our best front when meeting new people. What's this man like when he's having a bad day? Does Alfonso have a temper? What about his family? You say he's an entertainer and travels a lot. What would that mean for you? Will you travel with him? Or will you spend most of your time home alone, pining for him? And where will you live? I know you like to jump in boldly and discover things as you go, but there are too many unanswered questions. Questions that'll affect your long-term happiness."

"And yours." Ruby's expression had hardened as I spoke. "You won't have me to rely upon."

"What do you mean?"

"You'd be a lonely old maid if it weren't for me!"

I gaped at her. "I would not. Don't be foolish."

"I'm not foolish. I can be useful."

"Not foolish then but impulsive with your words and actions. You're indeed an asset, and I wouldn't want to be without you. What about your vision of us growing old together and having a house full of dogs?"

"That was a fantasy," Ruby said. "This is real life. My life, and I want a man in it. A man who loves me. And Alfonso does."

"He may have told you he does, but how has he shown it?"

"By proposing!"

I shook my head. "This holiday has made you lose your senses. I don't mind you indulging in a summer romance, but it has gone too far."

"You sound like a dour Victorian mother rather than my best friend," Ruby said. "You should support me. I'm happy."

"For a few brief moments, until you're left on your own when your new husband realises your family is virtually penniless and their country estate is falling into ruins. They may be entrepreneurs, but they're unsuccessful ones."

"That's untrue on both accounts. My parents have been going through a long sticky patch, but they'll come out the other side. And Alfonso would never abandon me because I'm not rolling in family money."

"Veronica, why don't you take five minutes?" Jacob suggested. "Emotions are running high, and you don't want to say anything else you'll regret."

"So far, I've regretted nothing," I said. "I speak the truth. Ruby just doesn't want to hear it because it'll burst her romantic bubble."

"You're speaking nonsense," Ruby said. "And you've ruined my day. I was so happy to receive the marriage proposal, and I wanted you to be the first to know. I wish I'd never bothered to come and tell you."

Benji whined and raised a paw, but I was too angry to settle him. Perhaps I had said one or two things in anger, but it made sense to me that Ruby had exaggerated her family's fortune, and this Italian Lothario thought he was onto a good thing. He planned on marrying her and then skipping away with a family fortune that didn't exist. Once Alfonso learned Ruby lived in a tiny flat with a shared bathroom, and her parents' country home was more suitable for the local vicar than the landed gentry, he'd be off. Ruby would be stuck with a broken heart and a marriage she couldn't get out of.

"I was going to suggest we all meet for dinner tonight. I planned on formally introducing you. Now, I won't. And none of you are invited to my wedding." Ruby huffed out a breath, tears in her eyes.

"Steady on. I insist on meeting this man," I said.

"No, it's not happening. You've insulted me, my family, and my fiancé. I'm thoroughly disappointed in you." Ruby turned on her heel and stomped away.

I stared after her, one hand settling on Benji's head as the realisation of my sharp words sank in. We rarely fell out, and never over a man. "I need to walk. Jacob?"

"So long as you don't go too fast. Perhaps we should try the pier?"

"A murder and a scandalous proposal have happened on that wretched pier. I want to go nowhere near it." I turned away from the pier and walked along the seafront. Although I desired to walk swiftly, it would mean Jacob was left behind, so I maintained a steady pace, Benji close to my heel.

"I understand that was shocking news, but you could have been gentler with Ruby," Jacob said.

"I can't be gentle when the situation is so dire. Ruby can be an absolute nincompoop when it comes to men, and this demonstrates it. If I hadn't been so busy looking at offices and investigating what happened to Emily, I wouldn't have missed the signs and could have put a stop to it."

"And looking after me, Edith, and Matthew," Jacob said. "Veronica, you can't help everybody. Ruby is a grown woman who makes her own decisions."

"I'm not sure she understands the dreadful decision she's just made, though. Marrying a stranger is unsettling. And getting out of that marriage won't be simple."

"Yes, it is. And it's something you'd never do," Jacob said. "But I'm not surprised when it comes to Ruby. She's always worn her heart boldly on her sleeve."

"Don't tell me you approve of this wedding?" I sidled around a group of seagulls squabbling over a dropped wrap of chips.

"It's not for me to approve or disapprove," Jacob said. "Perhaps Ruby has found her perfect man on the Margate sands."

I slid him a glare. "Are you suggesting I was unreasonable?"

"I'm suggesting you had a shock and need time to process the news before speaking to Ruby again."

"There's no time to process! If I'm to put a stop to this wedding, I must act now."

"Veronica, nobody is asking you to put a stop to anything," Jacob said. "Sometimes, we have to let people make mistakes. It's the only way they learn."

"I'm glad you see this marriage as a dreadful mistake."

"That's not what I meant. Ruby seems thrilled by this attachment. Naturally, you're concerned because it's happening fast and seems out of control, and we both know you love to control everything."

"You make me sound like a horror who won't allow anyone a lick of freedom."

"You sound like a woman who cares deeply about her friend and wants to do the right thing," Jacob said. "But sometimes, doing the right thing can involve standing back and letting other people make decisions you don't approve of."

I took several deep breaths. "No, there's only one thing for it."

"Are you going to find Ruby and apologise?"

"Absolutely not! We need to solve Emily's murder fast so I can knock sense into my best friend and then chase off the scoundrel who pretends marriage."

Jacob sighed. "The murder, of course. How do you plan on solving it?"

"We're going to another of Tommy's dancing shows and interrogating Ivy."

Chapter 16

"You haven't sat down since you came back this afternoon," my mother said. "I'm getting dizzy just looking at you whizzing about."

"There's much to do and too little time to do it." I paced from the window and freshened my mother's cup of tea.

"What are you talking about? This is supposed to be a relaxing holiday. Well, apart from the murder."

I sighed as I tidied my mother's stack of books. I hadn't been able to settle since my argument with Ruby. I also hadn't seen her since our disagreement. She'd most likely stormed off and into the arms of her new fiancé, complaining about what a terrible best friend I was. But I knew how to make things right. Once Ruby learned the truth about the man who'd proposed to her, whom I was convinced was devious and the very definition of a cad, she'd come to her senses and call the whole thing off. In order to have focused time to discover what a rotter he was, I needed to solve Emily's murder. Then, Ruby and her foolish heart would be my top priority.

"Veronica, didn't you hear me?" my mother asked.

I'd been so caught up in my thoughts that she could have told me the building was on fire, and I wouldn't have reacted. "My apologies. I have a lot on my mind."

"Is it Emily? Has new information come to light?"

"Nothing to solve the unsettling situation," I said. "We're discovering more suspects than we can discount."

"How perplexing," my mother said. "But you and Ruby always figure things out in the end. Where is that girl? With her charming young man, I suppose?"

My snort was most unladylike. I checked the time. I was due to meet Jacob and Bishop in the hotel lobby in five minutes. "I'll have to leave you to dine alone. We have a new lead to follow that can't be put off."

My mother waved away my comment. "I'll convince Matthew to come down with me. If he won't budge from his bed, I'll take dinner in his room. The dogs will keep us company. We'll want for nothing."

"If you do need anything, telephone the hotel lobby. They'll assist with any queries."

"I have stayed at a hotel before," my mother said. "And this trip is bringing back delightful memories of summer holidays I took with your father before the two of you were born. It seems like a lifetime ago."

"Over thirty years," I said.

"How swiftly the time passes."

"You are glad you came on this holiday, though?" I asked. "Memories can be bittersweet."

"I had my concerns, but it was the right thing to do," my mother said. "And I couldn't leave you unchaperoned. Even though Jacob was a police officer, men can be persuasive."

"He can be as persuasive as he likes around me, but he won't get anywhere," I said. "We're a long way from that sort of business."

My mother sighed. "I know. You're puzzling things out and taking your time. Sometimes, it's not so terrible to take a little risk, though."

I didn't agree, and the situation with Ruby proved my point. Risk created trouble and chaos for everybody else.

I pressed a kiss on my mother's cheek and patted Benji. "Enjoy your evening. I'll try not to be back too late."

"Enjoy yourself. I see they have sirloin on the menu tonight, so I think I'll treat myself. Perhaps a small glass of red wine, too. Although I shouldn't with the medication I'm on."

"One glass won't hurt. If you're asleep when I come back, I'll catch up with you in the morning." I collected my small handbag from my room, checking to see if Ruby had slipped in during my absence, but her things were untouched. She must return to the hotel eventually, or did she intend to spend the night with her new fiancé?

I had to put thoughts of Ruby to the back of my mind and focus on the investigation. Emily's killer was out there, and I was determined to find them and make sure they went behind bars for a very long time. I was glad of a focused conduit for my frustrations.

When I arrived in the hotel lobby, Jacob and Bishop were already there, clearly having arranged to meet earlier since they were both enjoying an ale.

"Am I late to the party?" I asked.

Bishop nodded a greeting. "No, we were catching up on old times and thought you'd be bored with police chat."

"I'd have found it most stimulating, but I'm glad you had the opportunity to catch up," I said. "Do we have access to the club this evening?"

"I was there earlier today, checking Tommy's alibi," Bishop said. "I made sure our names were on the guest list while I was there. It's one of Tommy's local venues, so it's close by. Less razzle dazzle and more acceptable to the tourists."

My eyebrows flashed up. "What about his alibi? Good news?"

"Good news for him," Bishop said. "Tommy is innocent."

I frowned. "Are you certain?"

"Veronica!" Jacob gently chided.

"Sorry, my nerves are on edge. Of course, you'd have done a thorough job checking the alibi."

"I asked some of the ladies at the club where Tommy was on the night of Emily's murder, and they confirmed he was there until gone one o'clock in the morning." Bishop finished his ale. "And he entertained a lady called Betty afterwards. They spent the night together. Tommy sometimes sleeps at the club."

"How romantic for Betty," I murmured.

"She's one of the dancers in Ivy's troupe," Bishop said. "A firecracker. She'll make sure Tommy shows her a good time."

"Perhaps such a good time that she's covering for him," I said as we made our way out of the hotel.

"If it was only her word, I'd agree with you," Bishop said. "But two more dancers confirmed it, and they have no special attachment to Tommy."

"Other than he's their employer," I said.

"Those girls are shrewd and take no prisoners," Bishop said, gesturing along the street. Since it was a pleasant evening, we were walking the short distance to the club. "And they wouldn't put up with a man turning on a woman. There is a code among these women, and if you break it, they come for you."

"Very well. Which leaves us with Ivy, your friend," I said.

"I must admit, I was shocked when Jacob told me what Lady Lizzie said about there being an argument between Ivy and Emily," Bishop said. "Ivy is another shrewd one, but I can't imagine she'd hide anything."

"She'd hide a lot of things if she killed Emily and was concerned you considered her guilty," I said. "Ivy wouldn't want her freedom taken away. And as you said, these ladies take no nonsense. What if Emily uncovered one of Ivy's secrets and confronted her? Ivy would have wanted it kept quiet. Emily didn't back down, so Ivy did the only thing she could to guarantee silence."

"I'm not convinced Ivy is involved, but we'll talk to her," Bishop said. "We need to hurry. The first performance will start soon, and we won't get the chance to talk to anybody until it's over."

There was a delay getting inside, with a long queue ahead of us, and we just arrived as the lights dimmed for the first performance. Chatting would be impossible while Ivy was in the middle of her shimmies and splits.

"We'll wait for the first act to end," Bishop said. "Then I'll get us an audience with Ivy."

We'd just settled in our seats when a flood of colour filled the stage. A chorus of dancing girls, feathers, and sequins swirled to the strident music. They were talented and flexible, legs flying and hips swaying. The mainly male audience was captivated.

After a few moments, I leaned over to Jacob. "I'll be back in a few moments. I need to find the toilet."

He nodded at me. "Don't go getting into trouble."

"I should say the same to you, the way you're eyeballing those ladies."

His cheeks flushed, and he looked away from the stage.

"I'm just teasing. Enjoy the show. I'll be back soon." Rather than visiting the toilet, I searched for a way to the dressing rooms the dancers used. They must have a backstage area where they prepared themselves and changed outfits. Not only did I want to find Ivy, but I also wanted to speak to Betty to confirm she'd been with Tommy on the night of Emily's murder. As I'd discovered with Ruby, love made a person do foolish things, like marrying a man they hardly knew. And I assumed the ladies would be more receptive to speaking with a female rather than two policemen. One current, one former.

It took a few moments of searching, but I discovered the dressing rooms past the toilet. If I got caught, I'd say I got turned around looking for the way back to the stage. As luck would have it, no one stopped me, and I soon heard the murmur of voices and soft laughter, the faint smell of perfume in the air.

I peeked my head around a red curtain to discover tables set with mirrors, adorned with all kinds of cosmetics, perfumes, and flimsy fabrics.

"You're in the wrong place if you need the loo," one of the ladies remarked, seeing me looking.

I pulled aside the curtain. "Thank you, but I know where I am. I'm Veronica. I'm looking for information about Emily Brewer's murder, and I wondered if you could assist."

"We don't give out information for free," another lady said.

"I'm happy to pay. Is one of you called Betty?"

All eyes swivelled to me, none of them friendly.

"What do you want with Betty?" A tall redhead in sparkly gold sequins stood from her seat.

"Are you Betty?" I opened my handbag and extracted my coin purse.

"You didn't answer my question," she said. "We don't want any trouble around here."

"Neither do I. But Emily was known to me, and I want to make sure her killer is caught. In particular, I'm interested in Tommy."

The redhead downed a shot of alcohol. "He's many things, but he ain't no killer."

"I'm learning Tommy is a complicated man," I said. "Emily got on his wrong side, and I fear the worst happened. If I could just get confirmation from Betty—"

"You'll get no confirmation from anyone." A leggy blonde joined the redhead. "You barging in here, flashing your money, and expecting us to scrape and grovel to your high-mannered ways. We know what the likes of you are all about."

"The likes of me?" I shook my head. "We've got off on the wrong foot. I'm here to help solve a crime."

"You're here with an expectation that we'd be scared of you and blab about our boss and who he's having dealings with," the blonde said. "Tommy looks after us. He gave some of us a job when no one else would. Everyone gets a second chance. He always says that."

"I'm happy to learn he's such a considerate employer," I said. "Is his relationship with Betty serious?"

The redhead smirked. "You're just like her. I remember Emily poking around and asking questions. Even after Tommy hired her to do a job for him, she kept coming back and bothering him."

"Did he give her a second chance when she annoyed him?" I asked.

"That's not what I meant! You posh types are all the same. You think you know the answers to everything, but you don't know how our lives work. Tommy is no killer."

"If I could just confirm his alibi with Betty, I'll be on my way," I said.

The redhead lunged at me and gripped my wrist tightly. "You're going nowhere. Tommy needs to know about this. And he won't be happy when he does."

I yanked my wrist away. "I want no trouble."

"Then you shouldn't have come back here making demands." She pulled a knife from her beaded purse.

I backed towards the curtain, but found one of the other dancers had snuck in and was blocking my escape. "It appears I've underestimated you ladies, and for that, I'm sorry. I meant no offence. I'm sometimes accused of being a touch blunt."

"Arrogant, more like," the redhead said. "It's time we taught you a lesson."

The curtain was pulled back, and Ivy appeared, dressed in red feathers and the skimpiest black outfit. "What's going on in here? Veronica!"

The redhead hesitated. "Do you know her?"

"In a manner of speaking." Ivy's curious gaze remained on me. "You're with Bishop's friend, aren't you? The handsome man with the limp."

I let out a sigh. "I am. And I appear to have made a mess of things with your friends."

"Ladies, simmer down," Ivy said. "If she knows Bishop, she's good people."

"She's nosy people. She was asking questions about Tommy and won't mind her business," the redhead said, swiftly hiding the knife.

"You come with me. Don't worry about this lot." Ivy took me by the elbow and led me out of the dressing room and along the corridor back towards the public area. The second we were out of earshot, she turned on me. "What do you think you're doing, messing around back here?"

"Looking for answers about Emily's murder," I said. "Bishop checked Tommy's alibi, but I wanted to make sure he'd missed nothing."

"Bishop never misses a thing," Ivy said. "You're lucky something didn't happen back there."

"Something almost did. I'm grateful you intervened."

"I did it to avoid washing blood out of my sequins," Ivy said. "Those girls have no manners. They were born fighting to survive, and they've never stopped. And they take offence when someone who is clearly born with a silver spoon in her mouth marches in and demands information."

I felt appropriately chastised. My head was less than clear, muddled with thoughts of Ruby's upcoming wedding, who killed Emily, and the expansion plans I had. It was too much. "I promise I won't bother those fine ladies again."

"I'm sensing a 'but.' Go on, what are you after?" Ivy settled a hand on one hip and arched an eyebrow.

"I just want a word with a dancer called Betty. She was with Tommy on the night of Emily's murder."

"I know they're close," Ivy said. "It's likely they were together that night."

"If I could just hear it from her, I'll go."

"You don't trust a man's word?"

"I ... only when I know him extremely well."

Ivy snorted a gentle laugh. "It's fortunate you amuse me. Stay there and don't move a muscle." She walked back to the dressing room and returned a few seconds later with a petite, dark-haired woman with full lips and Bambi-like eyes.

"You're Betty?" I asked.

"That's me." Betty darted a look at Ivy, who nodded at her. "I heard you were asking for me. I don't want any problems coming to my door if I say anything. And I don't have long until I'm on stage."

"Then I'll be direct. Did you speak to Inspector Bishop about Tommy's whereabouts on the night of Emily Brewer's murder?"

"Oh! That's what this is about," Betty said. "I was here with him. He's got a fancy room at the back he likes to entertain in. I could tell he was in the mood for romance after my dance, so I gave him a wink. We enjoyed each other's company. There's nothing wrong with that."

"Absolutely not," I said. "And you stayed all night?"

"As good as. I left at dawn," Betty said. "Tommy couldn't have harmed Emily. He was with me, and when I'm with a man, they only have thoughts and eyes for what I'm offering."

I believed her, which left me with a problem.

"Thank you, Betty. You can go." Ivy turned to me. "Now, you can go back to your civilised life and high teas and leave us working girls to it."

I hesitated. "What about you?"

Ivy had been walking back to the dressing room behind Betty. She stopped and pivoted. "What do you mean, me?"

"I've been made aware you argued with Emily shortly before her death."

"And?"

"Well, now she's dead. What did you argue about? Was it something serious?"

Ivy bared her teeth. "Ladies! We have a problem to deal with."

Chapter 17

"Ivy, you can trust me. I'm not here to cause you trouble," I said as I loosened the rope around my right wrist and slid my hand free. "You've had your fun. You can let me out." I'd been tied up and locked in a large cupboard for ten minutes.

On the other side of the closed door, the dancers were talking. I was a trifle concerned about my fate since one of them carried a knife, but I had backup, provided Jacob and Bishop could tear themselves away from the scantily clad ladies shimmying in front of them to come and find me.

"I know I didn't present myself well, but I'm harmless." I untied my left wrist and then my ankles, so I was free from the chair I'd been restrained in, and stood. "And I know my accent suggests I'm somewhat of a silver spoon, but I spent my life growing up in pubs. All over London and farther afield."

The voices on the other side continued, but I was certain they could hear me. I tiptoed around the room and quickly discovered the door was the only way out. The storage cupboard was full of some of the outlandish costumes the ladies wore for dancing. There were a variety of corsets, feather boas, and large feather fans. I grabbed a fan and waved it around my head. It was surprisingly heavy.

"I served in the war, too, so I've seen the darker side of life. Now I'm home, and I want to ensure that darkness doesn't creep into our communities." I was uncertain if my words were getting through. I set down the fan, unhooked a corset, and wrapped it around my middle. It was covered in green sparkly sequins.

There was a raised voice that sounded like Ivy then silence.

"I'm not a bad person. I adore animals. I volunteer my time at the dogs' home in Battersea. It's a marvellous place. And I have my own rescue dog, Benji. Unfortunately, Tommy's club doesn't allow animals inside. Otherwise, he'd be here, enjoying the show, too."

The voices had remained quiet. Was I finally getting through to them? There was a small mirror propped up against one wall, so I stood in front of it and examined myself in the corset, which I'd placed over my clothing. I wasn't sure I could pull off this look. I was more comfortable in practical clothes that I didn't mind getting muddy after a long walk with Benji.

I checked the time. Any moment now, Jacob would show up and scold me for sneaking off and trying to get answers without him being present. "I'm just a do-gooder, helping the police solve a murder. My apologies if I was too blunt, Ivy, but I have a dilemma to deal with, you see. A friend is about to marry an Italian stranger, and I must put a stop to it. But I have to solve Emily's murder first. You can understand why I was so plainspoken. I assumed you'd appreciate someone being straightforward and no-nonsense."

I turned to inspect how the corset looked from behind, and as I did so, a key turned in the lock, and Ivy yanked open the door. She took one look at me standing in front of the mirror in someone else's corset and burst into laughter. "Ladies, look at this. She's only gone and freed herself from the ropes and is getting dolled up."

Ivy's dancers crowded around behind her, several looking amused, although there were still some stony expressions.

"Oh, yes, sorry about that. I have thin wrists, you see. You should have made the knots tighter." I glanced down at the corset. "I hope you don't mind. I needed to keep myself entertained while I figured out what to do next."

Ivy let out another laugh and dabbed at an eye to stop a tear of amusement spoiling her makeup. "You're something else. It's as if you have no filter."

"It has been said before. I can barge around like a bull in a china shop to get what I want," I said. "Did you hear what I was saying?"

"Unfortunately, every word," the redhead said. "You're a hard one to keep quiet. We should have put a gag on you."

"That would have been unpleasant," I said. "But I understand why you'd consider it. I really do need to solve Emily's murder. Her aunt is devastated, so we must ensure justice is done."

"Mabel is a good egg. We often visit the Harbour Arms." Ivy set a hand on her hip. "Do you really consider me a suspect, though?"

I drew in a breath, realising I needed to tread carefully. "I have been given information about an argument you had with Emily."

Ivy's nostrils flared slightly. "Come out of there." I went to remove the corset, but she shook her head. "We'll give you a makeover while you're here."

"That's not necessary."

Ivy grabbed my arm, a steely look in her eyes. "I insist. We can glam you up while we talk."

Surrounded by half a dozen determined-looking women, several of them already reaching for their cosmetics, I decided not to argue.

"You're too thin for that corset," one of them said. "But we can pad it out."

"Just the makeup will be fine," I murmured.

"No, this is your punishment," Ivy said. "And it'll amuse me. You want to make sure I stay amused, don't you? You don't want to see my bad side."

Since I'd had a taste of Ivy's bad side, I acquiesced, being shuffled back into the changing room, undressed, shoved into the corset, provided with stockings and plenty of padding to go down the front of the outfit and a pair of high heels that I point-blank refused to wear.

I was met with more laughter as I came out of the dressing room, but Ivy shushed them. "Put some feathers on her, too, and she'll fit right in. We should get you up on the stage."

"I'm not one for dancing," I said. "And if I attempted the splits, I'd break something."

"We make what we do look easy," Ivy said, "but it takes a toll on the body. I can't imagine I'll be dancing for many more years."

"You'll be running this place one day," the redhead said.

Ivy smirked. "Sit here, Veronica. We'll paint you up."

I gritted my teeth and settled into the chair. Someone provided me with a large gin and tonic, which I was grateful for. Having a makeover was more stressful than being tied to a chair and locked in a room to await my fate.

"You really served in the war?" Ivy asked.

"I did. Communications to begin with."

"And after that?"

"A variety of things. I like to think I did my bit."

A knowing look crossed Ivy's face. "Same here. The war required all kinds of special services to get information out of the men in charge, if you know what I mean."

Given Ivy's profession, I had a good idea what services she'd employed, but I simply nodded. The Great War had been terrible, and we'd done things and got information in ways we weren't proud of to ensure this country's safety.

"You should have brought your dog," Betty said. "I love dogs. I have six at home. Chihuahuas. I sometimes bring them in and leave them here when I perform. Tommy doesn't like it, but they're no trouble."

"They are when they pee on the floor," the blonde said.

"Benji would adore meeting all of you," I said. "Your feathers would enchant him."

"We could do with something like that dogs' home you were talking about down here," Betty said. "We have a terrible problem with strays, and they're not treated kindly. I'm always on at our local councillor to sort something for them, but he's too busy having his palms greased to worry about a problem that won't make him money."

"Which councillor are you referring to?" I asked.

"Councillor Havisham. Nasty little man. Very sweaty. He often comes here on the weekend," Betty said. "I've danced for him a few times and always draw his attention to the stray animal problem, but he's only interested in looking at my cleavage."

"I met him when I was considering an office to rent. There was something about him I also didn't like. And Emily was researching a story involving Councillor Havisham. Something about fishing licences. Would you know anything about that?" I had to close my eyes as I was covered in fragrant powder.

"Fishing licences! I can only think Emily was looking into the trawler boys," Betty said.

"We have a regular party of fishermen who come to the club on their days off," Ivy said. "They're a rowdy bunch, but they spend well. And they like to treat us, which means they put money behind the bar, so Tommy always welcomes them."

"Fishing pays well?" I asked.

"The men work hard, and it's dangerous, but they only have to be on the boats for six months and then they take the rest of the year off. So yes, they earn a good living," Ivy said.

"And there's competition for the licences," Betty said. "I have one regular who complains about the increasing competition for getting a licence to fish. Without it, you can't go out in the waters."

"Councillor Havisham grants those licences?" I asked.

"For a hefty price," Betty said. "You're right not to trust him. He's involved in business development, but anyone can get a licence for just about anything if they pay him enough."

"Councillor Havisham takes bribes?" If Emily had been investigating the councilman for such a shady practice, he had the perfect motive for killing her. If she'd exposed him, his career would be over, his reputation ruined, and he'd most likely go to prison.

"What do you think?" Ivy stood back and looked at me in the mirror.

The reflection staring back at me was barely recognisable. My lips were bright red, my cheeks rosy, and I had so much eye makeup on that I could barely blink for fear of it falling off. "It's a different look. Theatrical."

"We need extra makeup under the heavy lights," Ivy said. "You could pass as one of us."

"If I decide on a career change, I'll come back and audition," I said.

Ivy laughed. "You do that. Stay here. I saw Bishop and your fancy man in the audience. They must be wondering what's going on." She walked away, returning a few moments later with a flustered-looking Bishop and Jacob, whose cheeks turned bright pink when he saw my state of undress.

"We've been looking for you," he said, not meeting my gaze.

"What have you been up to?" Bishop asked.

"Calm down, gentlemen," Ivy said. "There's no harm done. We had a few wrinkles to iron out, but as you can see, Veronica is one of us now."

Bishop looked at me and shook his head. "You should have been more careful."

"She was in my safe hands," Ivy said. "Although I wasn't best pleased when Veronica practically accused me of murdering Emily. As if I'd do such a thing."

"You never argued with Emily?" I asked.

Ivy exhaled slowly. "Ladies, give us a few moments, will you?"

The other women dutifully filed out, leaving me in the dressing room with Ivy, Bishop, and Jacob. Jacob's cheeks were still flushed.

Ivy pulled up a chair and sat beside me. "There was a disagreement. Emily learned I was helping Bishop with information gathering. She thought it was a good idea if I became her informant, too."

"And when you refused her, she got angry?" I asked.

"She was as hot-headed as I am," Ivy said. "I told her no, I wasn't interested, but she was persistent. Things got tense, and we had it out."

"When did this argument happen?" Bishop asked.

"Maybe a month ago," Ivy said. "I was taking a walk when she approached me on the beach one evening. I didn't think anyone else was around to see."

"You were seen," I said. "It must have been a heated argument for it to stick in someone's memory."

"It was. Emily wouldn't back down. As annoying as that was, I admired her for it. She even offered me money, as if I need that." Ivy shook her head. "After a while, she saw sense and realised I was no use to her and forgot the idea."

"That was the end of it?" I asked.

"It was. I told her it was too risky. I was already dancing with danger by speaking to Bishop," Ivy said.

"Why did Emily target you to become her informant?" Jacob asked.

Ivy pressed her lips together. "Emily was writing a story about Tommy. She knew I was close to him and thought she could get an inside scoop. But she was barking up the wrong tree."

"You're suggesting Tommy has no secrets?" I asked.

"Oh, he has plenty of secrets. He's no saint, but he's good for this town. He's a Margate lad, through and through. He gives back. He pays his workers well, looks out for his ladies, even donates to charity. Maybe you should ask him for a donation to set up a dogs' home down here. Betty would be thrilled."

"Yet he somehow launders money through his businesses and gets away with it," Bishop said.

Ivy smiled with a twinkle in her eye but said nothing.

Her words had me almost convinced she was innocent. Ivy was as straight-talking as me. "Bishop, have you thoroughly checked Ivy's alibi for the night of Emily's murder?"

Ivy bristled but then rolled her eyes. "Of course, he checked. I've already told you, he knows what he's doing. I can figure a man out in the blink of an eye, and Bishop is as honest as my stockings are long and silky."

"It's been checked," Bishop acknowledged.

"Ivy couldn't have crept out of the party to the pier at any point?"

"You're pushing your luck," Ivy said. "I've told you the absolute truth. I am sorry for what happened to Emily, but I'm not surprised she found herself in a heap of trouble. She didn't have the backup to be so pushy. I can speak my mind and get away with most things because I have Tommy looking out for me, my ladies, and Bishop. The same goes for you, Veronica. You have your friends and now Bishop watching your back when you get uppity. Others aren't so fortunate. Emily was fearless, looking to uncover the truth without worrying about the consequences. Look where it got her."

Betty poked her head into the room. "Sorry to disturb you, Ivy. You're on in two minutes."

"Thanks. I've got to go. Sorry about tying you up," she said to me.

"I deserved it. And if I get an opportunity, I'll show you a more effective knot, so next time, I won't escape."

Ivy chuckled. "There'd better not be a next time." She slid a hand across Bishop's chest as she walked past him and out of the room.

"Give me a few minutes to get changed and we can leave." I slipped into the large storage cupboard and shimmied out of the uncomfortable corset and stockings. I removed the makeup as best I could, put on my much more suitable dress, and then rejoined the gentlemen. "Shall we?"

We walked out of the club in silence, Ivy already performing on stage to a gaggle of bright-eyed men.

Once we were in the fresh air, Jacob turned to me, frustration glowing on his face. "That was a big risk. I can't take my eyes off you for five minutes before you get yourself in trouble."

"I thought if I spoke to the ladies on my own, they might be more receptive," I said. "But I made a mistake and put my foot in it."

"And they tied you up?" Jacob shook his head.

"It all came good in the end," I said. "And we now have one less suspect to consider."

Bishop puffed out a breath. "You're fortunate you found Ivy in a good mood."

"Once you scratch the surface, we have a great deal in common," I said. "I met a like-minded soul, and we bonded."

"After she tied you up," Jacob said.

"Stop fretting about that. It was something and nothing."

Jacob looked like he wanted to continue the debate but not in front of Bishop.

"Since we've discounted Doctor Patterson, Tommy is out of the picture, and now Ivy is in the clear," Bishop said, "who does that leave us with?"

I smiled. "Once I got the ladies talking, they told me something fascinating about Councillor Havisham. Our councillor is in the business of taking bribes, and I believe Emily wanted that stopped."

Both men looked startled.

"So he killed her?" Bishop's expression grew perplexed. "How? He's old and slow."

"But perhaps determined enough to ensure his grubby secret wasn't exposed." I turned towards the hotel. "Tomorrow, we pursue a new suspect."

Chapter 18

My mother sat in front of an untouched plate of eggs and toast at breakfast the next morning, looking pensive. Matthew sat beside her, grimly determined, his head down as he ate a sausage.

"Why didn't you say something sooner?" my mother finally said.

"I would have done, but I've been processing the shocking news." I glanced at Jacob, who was deliberately keeping out of the conversation about Ruby's inappropriate love match and upcoming wedding. "I hoped it was some dreadful joke she'd taken too far."

"Marriage isn't a joke," my mother said. "I'll admit, this Italian chap is terribly handsome, but she can't marry him! And certainly not here. There's no time to prepare."

"The getting prepared part is the least of our worries," I said. "We know nothing about this man."

"Maybe he makes Ruby happy," Matthew muttered. "Is it our place to interfere?"

"She's my best friend, and I know when she's making a mistake," I said. "What if they marry and he whisks her off to Italy? We'll never see her again."

"Unless you want Ruby to learn you're gossiping about her, you need to change the subject," Jacob said. "She's coming this way."

I shot out of my seat in surprise at the sight of Ruby striding towards us, her usually sunny expression set to grim. "Where have you been?"

"I stayed at a different hotel." Ruby sat in an empty seat and helped herself to toast. "I needed time to cool off after our last conversation."

I settled back in my seat, perching on the edge. "And have you cooled off?"

She shot me a sharp look. "Have you?"

Jacob briefly pressed a hand on my knee underneath the table.

"My shock made me blurt out inappropriate things. I am sorry if I hurt your feelings," I said.

"You accused my husband-to-be of only marrying me because of my family connections. Connections I elaborated, so he'd be interested in me," Ruby said.

"Yes, that was regrettable."

"Unforgivable, more like," Ruby said. "I was hoping you'd be my bridesmaid, but now I'm not so sure. Perhaps I'll ask Mabel. That'll cheer her up."

"Mabel would make a fetching bridesmaid," I said. "May I just say one thing?"

"I'm sure you have plenty of questions, and I can't stop them," Ruby said. "Go ahead. One question."

"Why the rush? Come back to London, choose a venue there, and take time to make plans."

"I don't want to wait," Ruby said. "This is a new chapter of my life, and I'm embracing it. It's a delicious whirlwind."

"Whirlwinds cause damage." I hurried on. "Was it your choice or his to have such a speedy wedding?"

"There you go. That's more than one question," Ruby said. "We decided together. As a couple. Edith, you must be happy for me. You're very welcome to attend the wedding."

My mother appeared cautious as she twisted her linen napkin. "Whirlwind romances can work, but you must be certain he's the right one for you."

"I knew the second I laid eyes on him," Ruby said.

"What tosh," I said.

Ruby frowned at me. "Tosh? Are you saying that because of your lack of romantic bones? You don't understand. I don't know why I bothered coming to see you."

"Wait." I reached over and grabbed her arm. "Don't go. Let's talk about the wedding. And we must arrange to meet your fiancé."

"To assess his suitability, I suppose."

"If he's a part of your life, then he's a part of ours," I said. "That is, unless you're disappearing off to Italy the moment you wed."

Ruby's stiffness softened a fraction. "There are no plans for us to go anywhere. Not in the short term. Alfonso is excited to see my home, and he wants to meet Lady M's horses. He rides. Did I tell you that?"

"You've told me barely anything about him," I said. "Which is why we must meet him before you marry."

"All you need to know is he's smashing, rich, and has two homes in Italy."

"Goodness. Two homes! Does he have a big family?" my mother asked.

"Huge. I've always wanted to be a part of a large family," Ruby said.

"You have numerous siblings," I said. "Isn't that big enough?"

"They're scattered. I barely see them."

That wasn't true, but now wasn't the time to debate with Ruby.

"Why is Alfonso in Margate?" I asked.

"I told you. He's an entertainer. He goes where the work is. And since Margate's been blossoming with growing tourism numbers, he found the perfect seasonal job for his talents."

"Doesn't his seasonal work concern you?" I asked. "You could end up doing an awful lot of travelling just to see each other. And he must work nights. That could be difficult."

"We've discussed it, and we're figuring things out," Ruby said. "We'll make it work. Love always finds a way."

"It seems suspicious that he'd swap Venice for Margate," I said. "Surely, there's work for him in Italy."

"I didn't say he lived in Venice," Ruby said. "But why not Margate? We came here for a holiday. If it's good enough for us, it should be acceptable to him. You're looking for faults and problems when there are none to uncover."

"Perhaps we should talk about something else," Jacob said. "Maybe Emily's murder. It's a more cheerful subject."

I speared him with a glare.

"Solving a murder and planning a wedding during our holiday," my mother said. "This is hardly the peaceful time you promised us, Veronica."

"Neither were on my agenda," I said. "But sometimes, these things can't be helped."

"I wish I could help," Ruby said on a sigh, "but with the wedding only days away, I already have so much to deal with."

"I'd offer to assist," my mother said, "but my feet are playing up again. I was planning a restful day in my room. I have a new book to read. Colonel Griffin gave it to me."

"I've accepted I'm on my own with the preparations." Ruby slid me a pointed look. "The wedding is on Friday at two pm at the town hall. I'll leave it up to you if you wish to be there. If you'll excuse me, I must get on with my day." She pushed back from the table and strode away.

"Oh dear. What a pickle," I said. "The sooner we solve this murder, the quicker we can drag Ruby away from making the biggest mistake of her life."

Matthew sucked in a breath. "What if she isn't? You're so quick to judge."

"I ... Well, perhaps I can be a little fast, but I like to think I have an open mind," I said.

Jacob attempted to hide a smile behind his napkin. "Your brother has a point. You do a good job with strangers, but not so much with the people who are close to you."

I looked around the table. I could be harsh on those I loved most dearly. I compared them to my own exacting standards. I recognised it was a tiny character flaw.

"We will go to the wedding, won't we?" my mother asked. "You'll regret it if you don't."

I didn't want there to be a wedding. I wanted Ruby to come to her senses. "We'll see. Murder first."

My mother finally found her appetite and tucked into her eggs. "How did your evening go? Was the new lead a success?"

"A roaring success." I decided to leave out the details of our adventures in Tommy's club so as not to jangle my mother's nerves. "Emily had uncovered a corruption scandal in the local council. One of the councilmen is taking bribes in exchange for business licences. We need to find a way to speak to him and confront him."

"A respected member of the community committing murder," my mother exclaimed. "This world is a broken place."

"Stranger things have happened, but we must be swift in pursuing this," I said. "You have your plans for the day with a book, so you won't be bored. But what about you, Matthew?"

"I'm planning on hiding in my room, too."

I sighed. "You will take Felix for a walk, though?"

"I took him out at dawn. It's quiet then. I like seeing the sun come up."

And Matthew liked the fact there were no people about at dawn. I decided not to push them. We were getting to the end of this holiday, and the cracks were showing in all of us.

"After breakfast, I'm off to speak to Bishop," Jacob said. "I'll see if he's got any dirt on Councillor Havisham, or if he has an in with him so we can get him talking."

"And I need to take Benji for a long walk. I've been neglecting him," I said. The walk wasn't only for his benefit, but also for mine. I needed a clear head to tackle these problems, and there was nothing like bracing sea air to clear the sinuses and murky thoughts.

After we'd finished our breakfast and gone our separate ways, I headed out in a new direction with Benji. I enjoyed exploring new areas. Margate had wonderful little streets tucked away from the main routes, with adorable cottages featuring tiny windows and low door frames. They must have once been fishermen's cottages.

I headed away from the residential area, and fifteen minutes later, we found ourselves walking towards boat moorings. There were dozens of boats of various shapes and sizes lined up, gently bobbing on the waves.

Benji froze, one paw in the air, his nose up and his tail straight out behind him.

"Have you picked up a scent?" I asked him.

His hackles rose slightly just as a large, rough-coated grey dog shot out from behind an upturned box and barked at us.

"There's nothing to worry about, old boy. Benji is quite friendly, and so am I." I hunted in my handbag for a few seconds and found treats, which I threw to the dog. He hesitated for a second and then gobbled them down. The barking descended to a low grumble.

"That's more like it. What's wrong with your paw?" The dog held his right front paw slightly off the ground, as if it troubled him to put weight on it.

"Stop bothering that lady," a man yelled from one of the boats. It took me a moment to locate him, but then I spotted a man of around fifty with a grizzled face and a grey beard, similar in colour to his dog's fur. He had a cap on his head and wore dark blue stained overalls.

"Is he yours?" I called out.

"He's not supposed to be off the boat. Get back here, Banjo."

"Banjo! What a sweet name. This is Benji, and I'm Veronica." I crouched cautiously and held out a hand. After a moment, Banjo sniffed me. Supplying several more treats even got his tail wagging.

By this time, the man had clambered off the boat and strode over. "Sorry if he frightened you, missus."

"That's quite all right. I'm used to dogs. I've had Benji for some time, and I volunteer at an animal rescue. We get all sorts of characters showing up there."

"Do you, now? Not from around here, are you?"

"No, I'm from London," I said. "Veronica Vale."

"Colin. And as you've probably figured out, that's Banjo. He's always off hunting for food, even though he gets plenty of fish from me."

"You're a fisherman?" I asked.

"My family has been in the seafaring business for generations," Colin said. "I inherited the boat from my father when he passed."

I looked at the boat. I knew little about seafaring vessels, but it was attractive, painted in blue and white with the name Jolly Salty on the side. "It's a fine vessel."

"It serves its purpose. We'd better be off before we get in your way."

"Before you go, I noticed Banjo's paw is troubling him. Has he recently had an injury?"

Colin scowled and scraped a hand through his beard. "He won't let me look at it. He's been limping for days. I was hoping he just sprained it, but it could be something more serious."

"Do you have a local vet who could assist?"

"He's on holiday."

"Would Banjo let me take a look if I gave him more treats?" I asked.

"You can try, but I can't promise he won't give you a nip."

"Perhaps we could take this on board your boat?" I suggested. "Banjo might feel more confident in familiar surroundings. It would also be easier to hold him in one place rather than have him skitter away behind an empty container."

Colin considered the offer and then nodded. "I don't like to think of him suffering. Right this way. You'll have to excuse the smell of fish. It comes with the job."

"Trust me, I've experienced much more pungent smells over the years."

Colin gave me a curious look but asked no questions, holding out his hand to assist me onto the boat. Benji and Banjo hopped nimbly on board, Benji seeming right at home, even though I'd never taken him on a boat of any description.

Colin took us below deck into a tidy, slightly fishy scented living space. I settled on a seat, more treats in my lap, and spent a few minutes getting to know Banjo, talking to him gently and scratching behind his ears. Once he was relaxed, I reached for his injured paw. He flinched, but another treat convinced him the indignity would be worth it.

I lifted the paw and instantly saw a swollen pad. Gently easing two claws apart, I discovered a splinter of wood.

"Do you see the problem?" Colin lurked nearby, concern on his face.

"Yes, and although Banjo may not like it, I need to do an extraction. Would you be so good as to hold his head in case he gets feisty?"

Colin got into place, keeping a firm grip on Banjo's head, while I whipped out the splinter and sat back. Banjo squirmed, but made no attempt to bite either me or Colin. He licked his paw for a few seconds and then wagged his tail.

"This was your culprit!" I held up the large splinter. "He must have stood on it while nosing around those containers out there."

"That'll teach him not to be so greedy." Colin appeared relieved. "Thank you, missus. I've never seen him take to a person so quickly. You must have a good way about you. Animals always know when to trust a person."

"The treats helped." I looked around the boat. "This must be quite a tough existence."

Colin settled into the seat opposite me, relaxed now I'd helped Banjo. "It is. But there are new permits coming along soon, which means more days out fishing. That'll be good news for everybody. At least everybody who can afford a new licence."

"Your family has always worked out of Margate?" I continued patting Banjo, alternating between giving him and Benji treats to ensure he didn't feel left out.

"Fishing is in our blood," Colin said. "It's all I've known. We're most likely descended from pirates!"

"Banjo, too?"

"He loves being on the open water. Neither of us is made for the land."

"Colin, are you down there? Don't think you can hide from me."

Colin jerked in his seat and then rolled his eyes. "I forgot he was coming by."

I recognised the voice. "Is that Councillor Havisham?"

Colin was already pulling out a bulky envelope from his inside jacket pocket. "Yes. Do you know him?"

"We've met. What is he doing here?"

"Colin! Where are you?" Councillor Havisham called again.

"Down here, sir," Colin yelled back then muttered to me, "What a blethering nuisance."

Councillor Havisham descended the wooden steps. "You're two days late paying. Don't think I won't give your licence to someone else if I don't get my money."

Colin scowled as Councillor Havisham appeared. "I've got it. Just as I promised."

I stood and crossed my arms over my chest, a flicker of delight running through me. The second Councillor Havisham saw me, he froze, and his cheeks flushed as he realised he'd been caught red-handed, about to take a bribe.

Chapter 19

"Miss Vale! I ... what a pleasant surprise." Councillor Havisham was already backing up the steps. "Colin, I didn't realise you had company. I'll come back later."

"Don't you want your money?" Colin appeared bemused at the councilman's odd behaviour.

I wasn't. Margate's local pillar of the community had been caught with his hand in the biscuit tin, stealing all the cream-filled bourbons. "Please, don't go on my account. I was learning some fascinating information about fishing licenses."

Colin slid me a startled look. "I thought you were just indulging an old codger. What's a nice lady like you want to do with smelly boats and slimy fish?"

"Why don't you tell him, Councillor Havisham?" I marched to the bottom of the wooden steps. "Or should I assume the money Colin offered you is a charitable donation and not a bribe to ensure his license isn't taken from him?"

His face shifted chameleon-like through several shades of red before settling on a mottled fuchsia with an undertone of damson jam. "Bribe? Bribe! How dare you. I'm a respected member of the community. I've brought more business into this town than you've had hot dinners."

"And most likely accepted bribes from most of those business owners." I wasn't letting him get away with this. This bluster and indignation may work on some, but I'd got a hint of how he operated when I met him at the office. Jacob and I could have secured any venue we desired for the right price. And most of that price would have been tucked into Councillor Havisham's back pocket. It was shocking behaviour. Behaviour he'd have killed for to keep someone quiet.

Colin lowered his outstretched hand. "Does this mean I don't have to pay?"

Councillor Havisham gulped as he looked at the money. He fixed his gimlet glare on me. "I sense the whiff of a scandal."

"The only thing I smell is fish and fakery," I shot back.

"What's an unmarried woman—and I know you're not committed to Mr Templeton—doing on her own with a rough-handed working man." A slippery smile crossed Councillor Havisham's face.

"Your words and veiled accusations won't make me run," I said. "I've looked a German soldier in the eye while he held a gun to my head and not backed down. I intend to do the same thing with you."

A flash of confusion crossed Councillor Havisham's face. "Stuff and nonsense. As is the fanciful idea that I take bribes. My record is clean."

"Only because you've never been caught," I said. "Colin, how long has this been going on?"

He looked at me. "My license payments?"

"The extra money Councillor Havisham personally takes from you to ensure you can continue fishing. You do know this is illegal?"

Colin scratched at his beard. "He said it was a guarantee. Like an insurance. We all pay it. It's the top up guarantee, isn't that right, sir?"

Councillor Havisham choked out a strangled laugh. "Pay no attention to Colin. He's a simple man of the sea. I always give my constituents special attention when they need help, if you understand me."

"Completely. You exploit desperate people who need to keep their businesses by making up fake guarantees and demanding payment for them. If I were to examine the council's accounts, these payments wouldn't be listed, would they?"

"You'd never be allowed to do such a thing. Women have no head for numbers."

"We have a head for discovering crooks, and you're one of them." I drew in a breath. "And that's not all you are."

"I don't like the meaning behind those words." Councillor Havisham's expression hardened. "What are you suggesting?"

Benji softly growled, and Banjo joined him.

"Keep those creatures under control." Councillor Havisham backed up. "I came here to support you, Colin, not to be insulted and threatened."

"I really am lost. Does that mean you don't want your money?" Colin asked. "I'm sorry I couldn't make the usual meeting, but I had to make an emergency repair on the boat. I told one of the others to let you know."

"Do be quiet," Councillor Havisham snapped.

"When did your usual meeting take place?" I jumped on Colin's revelation.

"We were supposed to meet the night the new amusements opened," Colin said. "Ten of us to hand over the extra payments. We do it four times a year. It's our guarantee payments. Isn't that right, sir?"

"That's not what happened." Councillor Havisham was sweating, and it wasn't because of our confined, fishy quarters.

"What time were you supposed to meet?" I asked.

"Just before midnight. I always thought it was a strange time to conduct business, but better that than lose my license." Colin's eyes widened. "Did I say something wrong?"

"No, Colin. You've been most helpful." I arched an eyebrow at Councillor Havisham. "So much for you being at a work meeting late and then returning home. Did you think you could keep your lie a secret?"

"I wasn't lying! And I was at a meeting that evening. Colin is mistaken."

Colin shook his head. "You can ask the other fellas. They were all there."

"Thank you. I shall," I said.

"Keep your nose out of my business." Councillor Havisham glared at me before shifting his fury to Colin. "You'll find my licence quota is full, and your name isn't on the list."

"Hold on now! I have your money." Colin waved the envelope. "Take it!"

"I don't know what that is."

"Councillor Havisham, we need to visit the police station. You have questions to answer," I said. "Questions about what you did after you took the money. Did you happen to visit the pier?"

He hovered by the wooden steps then turned and fled.

I sighed. Why did they always run? "Benji, if you'd do the honours."

Benji took off like a rocket, Banjo close behind him. A few seconds later, there was a yelp, followed by a large splash.

Colin stared at me. "What just happened? Am I in trouble?"

I smiled at him. "You've done nothing wrong. But hold on to that money and expect a visit from the police. Now, if you'll excuse me, I have a sodden councillor to fish out of the sea."

I raised my glass of gin fizz, only pausing for a second to see if Ruby would appear in the dining room doorway to join us. I hadn't seen her since our disastrous breakfast earlier that day. "Here's to catching the killer."

"And almost drowning the beggar." My mother sat to one side of me, Matthew the other, and Jacob opposite. I'd also invited Bishop to join us in the merriment, but he was busy tidying the loose ends of Emily's murder investigation. The main loose end being charging the thieving, scheming Councillor Havisham with her death.

"It was a fitting capture," Jacob said.

"We have Benji and his new friend Banjo to thank for that." Benji was contentedly snoozing in my hotel room, most likely dreaming of chasing bad men and pushing them into the sea to see how big of a splash they made.

"And it took four burly men to fish him out! Veronica, are you sure that's correct?" my mother asked. She'd heard the story from me three times but still kept asking me to repeat it.

I nodded. "I was there when it happened. It appears some of his illegally gained funds were spent on lavish dinners, and plenty of them."

"By tomorrow morning, all of Margate will know Councillor Havisham is out of a job and going to prison for the rest of his life," Jacob said.

My mother tutted. "Shame on him. Hurting a sweet girl like Emily to keep his shabby little lies hidden. If Benji hadn't bitten him, I'd send him over to teach the scoundrel a lesson."

"It wasn't Benji who nipped the councillor; it was Banjo. They made an excellent pair," I said.

"And the fisherman, Colin, is happy to tell everything to the police?" Matthew had listened quietly but intently as I'd updated the family on the investigation.

"Colin is angry and feels foolish at being caught out by Councillor Havisham," I said. "He genuinely believed he was supposed to pay extra money to keep his fishing licence. Colin makes an excellent living off the sea, so he assumed, and the councillor told him, that he had to pay a percentage of his profits directly to him. He called it an insurance guarantee, but it was all a con."

"I expect Councillor Havisham will be glad to be behind bars," Jacob said. "Having a dozen or so burly, angry fishermen chasing him to get their money back would make any man blanch."

"They won't get back a penny," my mother said. "I expect he spent it on cheap women and expensive champagne."

"Councillor Havisham isn't saying what he spent the money on," Jacob said, "but Bishop is looking into his financial dealings. He'll uncover what happened. The only sticking point is that Councillor Havisham is refusing to confess to Emily's murder."

I nodded. "Bishop mentioned he's being truculent."

"It must have been him. The harbour where the fishing boats dock isn't far from the pier," Jacob said. "It would have been easy for Councillor Havisham to collect the bribes and then walk to the pier. He must have arranged to meet Emily there."

"Or he saw her taking an evening walk," my mother said. "He knew she wouldn't let the story go, so he snuck after her. He hoped he'd be able to push her off the pier and get away with it, but she fought back."

"We'll find injuries on him," I said. "Even without a confession, we've got enough evidence to convict him."

We sipped our drinks and waited until our food was served before continuing the conversation.

"I thought Mabel was joining us?" my mother asked.

"She found even more of Emily's journals in the loft," I said. "She wanted to sort through them before she came to the hotel. She said she wouldn't be long."

"And still no Ruby back with us?"

"No Ruby," I muttered.

"It's good Mabel is getting out," my mother said cheerfully. "We don't want her stuck in the pub feeling miserable."

"She'll have mixed emotions," I said. "Mabel now knows who killed Emily, but that doesn't bring her back."

"Wretched men and their scheming," my mother said. "I hope you don't have any schemes up your sleeve, Jacob. Veronica needs a simple man in her life."

I failed to hide my laugh. "Jacob is anything but simple. Grumpy, often. Sharp with his words when I'm doing something adventurous, most definitely. But never simple."

"If you don't mind me saying, Mrs Vale, Veronica needs a man who'll keep her on her toes or she'll grow bored," Jacob said.

My mother sighed. "Her father was just the same. I kept telling him to slow down and stop taking risks, but I knew who I was marrying. And I'd never have been content with a man who liked a pipe and slippers and his dinner served at the table by five pm every night while the radio played in the background. We sometimes lived in chaos, but it was always happy, wasn't it?"

"Mostly, it was blissful," I said. "Oh look, there's Mabel now. She'll be able to order a main course, and we can all eat together."

Mabel dashed towards the table with a small box under her arm. She had the air of someone who had a million and one things on her mind.

"I'm so glad you could make it." I stood and pulled out an empty seat for her.

"I'm not here to eat. I wish I could put my feet up, but two of my bar staff have called in sick, so it's just me and one young girl dealing with things. Not that I worry, mind. I prefer keeping busy."

"Having a purpose during a difficult time is helpful," I said. "Can you not even stay for a swift drink?"

Mabel smiled. "I have enough of that where I work. Thank you for the offer, though. And thank you so much for finding out what happened to Emily. I had a visit from Bishop, and according to the fishermen he's interviewed, it's been going on for years. Those poor fellas thought they were paying extra to get exclusive rights or some such nonsense. All this time, Councillor Havisham has been cheating them and pocketing the money."

"We were just talking about the dreadful situation," my mother said.

"And Emily found out what was going on and planned to put a stop to it," Mabel said. "She was such a good girl."

"Did Emily ever talk to you about Councillor Havisham? Mention any concerns about the way he treated local businesses?" I asked.

"She talked about some of her stories and kept teasing me about a big one she wanted to crack wide open, but she needed more evidence."

"Perhaps Emily was hoping to get an interview with a fisherman," Jacob said. "Although they may have been reluctant to talk to someone so young."

I nodded. "And female. Colin was unwilling to speak to me until I assisted with Banjo's injured paw, and then we became the best of friends."

"Don't take it to heart," Mabel said. "Our men of the sea have old-fashioned values. They work so hard to provide for their families. The women stay home and raise the children, and the men do all the dangerous work."

"I'd wager raising children comes with its fair share of danger," I murmured.

"Good for them," my mother said. "I can't imagine anything worse than being out on a blustery sea attempting to pull in huge nets full of flailing fish. Imagine the stench!"

I thought briefly that it could be interesting, but having spent almost two weeks in Margate, surrounded by a flurry of fishy delights, I'd come to realise my palate wasn't meant for seafood.

"I can't stay any longer," Mabel said. "But thank you again. I thought you might like these. It's the last of the boxes full of Emily's notepads. She was always researching someone or other."

I took the box. "Thank you. Are you sure you don't want to keep any of these to remember Emily by?"

"I've got a flat and a pub full of memories of Emily. She won't be forgotten. Some of my regulars are putting together a frame of photographs of her. She was often seen striding around town and talking to anyone she could stop. Always looking for a story, that one."

Unfortunately, Emily had found the biggest story in Margate, and it had cost her her life. Still, I admired her. When I discovered a fascinating trail, I always followed it, despite people telling me not to do so.

Mabel dabbed away a rogue tear. "Enjoy your meal. Will you stop by the pub before you go back to London?"

"I'll be sure to do that," I said. "We'll have a drink and raise a glass to Emily."

Mabel swept away another tear. "I'd like that. She would too. She thought so highly of you. I remember her telling me she wanted to be just like Veronica Vale."

"She wasn't far behind me," I said. "And I know she was a local Kent lady, but I'd be honoured to put an obituary in the London Times. Give Emily the appropriate send-off. That way, there'll always be a record of her in the files."

"She'd love that. And so would I. Send me a copy when it's published." Mabel gave us all a wave and dashed out of the dining room.

The next two hours were spent enjoying a leisurely dinner: three courses, a whole bottle of wine, followed by coffee and mints. It was most indulgent, but everyone was in a jubilant mood after Emily's murder had been solved and the crooked criminal taken off the streets.

By the time I headed up the stairs, Matthew in front of me assisting our mother, and Jacob beside me, I was stifling a yawn.

"Have you made a decision about Ruby?" Jacob asked softly so my mother wouldn't overhear.

"I still want to shake sense into her," I said. "And this continual disappearing act does no one any good."

"You do think she'll return to the hotel, don't you?" Jacob asked.

"She can't stay away for much longer. Ruby has a limited purse," I said.

"Perhaps her new fiancé is assisting her. He could have lodgings here."

"She said she was staying in a different hotel." I grimaced. "I certainly hope they haven't already formed a household. That would complicate things."

Jacob remained silent until we reached the top of the stairs. "May I suggest a different approach?"

"The approach I'm taking is perfect," I said. "If I have to drag Ruby kicking and screaming back to London, then so be it."

"And lose her friendship for good?"

"When she's away from the bright lights of Margate and the heady delights of a long sunny holiday, she'll realise what a mistake she's made," I said.

"And if she doesn't? Are you prepared for that?"

I chewed on my bottom lip as I stopped by my hotel room door. "I'm prepared to keep my best friend safe. Good night, Jacob."

After another pause, he bid me goodnight and headed to his own room. I entered my room and was warmly greeted by Benji. I unfolded the napkin I'd snuck out of the dining room and fed him a small piece of steak. Once that had been devoured, I prepared myself for bed and sat up for a few moments, reading a book. I was tired, but my mind raced. Even though the murder was solved, there was so much else to think about.

Was I taking on too much? I had a busy life in London. Would expanding it into another county with Jacob break me? I shook my head. I was made of stern stuff and had got through a war in one piece. I could handle a little extra work and, if necessary, employ people to assist.

I settled down in bed, Benji on the floor, and closed my eyes. Twenty minutes of tossing and turning proved sleep wouldn't come easily. I sat up and turned on the light again, reaching for the small box Mabel had given me containing Emily's notebooks. I pulled one out and flicked through it. It was more of her almost illegible scribblings. I pulled out another one. A pretty notepad with flowers printed on the front.

I made myself a soothing cup of tea and settled back on the bed with the notepad. Benji hopped up beside me and rested his head on my knee. I gently ran my fingers through his fur as I sipped my tea and attempted to decipher Emily's notes.

She had a habit of writing a single word and circling it several times as if for emphasis. The word she kept coming back to time and again was 'development.' Could this relate to Councillor Havisham? She knew he was developing plans to take more money from the fishermen?

That wasn't it. I'd seen Emily's notes about Councillor Havisham. She'd focused on fishing and licences, not development. Did she mean building development?

I turned the page and saw a name circled repeatedly. As I slowly deciphered Emily's scrawling hand that swirled around the focus word, I almost dropped my cup of tea.

Councillor Havisham wasn't the killer.

Chapter 20

The sun was barely peeking above the horizon the next morning as I paced past my hotel room window. I'd watched the moon all night as it slid away to admit its burning companion, waiting for the world to awaken so I could put this mystery to bed and get justice for Emily.

Benji walked beside me, my ever-faithful companion, no matter the time. His head was down, sensing the seriousness of last night's discovery.

My head was also lowered as I clutched Emily's notepad. "How could I have been so foolish?"

I'd muttered the same words over and over. Had I been fooled by helpful words and a pleasant voice? Or were my other distractions ensuring my sleuthing skills had slipped? If I was to open a successful private investigation agency with Jacob, that could never be allowed.

Benji nudged me with his head, bringing me back, and my gaze shifted to the window.

"That's good enough. The day has begun. We'll get your breakfast and then head to the archive."

Benji wagged his tail at the prospect of not only food, but also a brisk walk.

Before I could prove anything, I needed to gather facts. And I'd been thrilled to discover a large public archive in the centre of Margate. That would have everything I needed for the final pieces of this puzzle to slide into place.

I could handle nothing more than a strong cup of tea, but the staff warmly obliged Benji with a bowl of food. I did my best not to tap my foot while he ate. It would do no good to give my companion indigestion.

With Benji still licking his chops, we dashed outside. The sea air was bracing and cleared the cobwebs that a lack of sleep often weaved. Turning off the seafront, we hurried past pretty shops and several adorable cafes, just opening for the day to take in deliveries.

A flight of steps led to the archive's entrance. I reached the door and frowned. "Drat! They don't open until nine."

Benji cocked his head.

"This won't wait! We must get inside."

"Is there something I can do you for, missus?" A rotund woman carrying a bucket stopped by the steps.

"Perhaps. Do you work here?" I asked.

She nodded. "I clean. You can't get inside yet. Not for two more hours."

"Could you make an exception? This is a matter of justice!"

The woman clambered the steps. "Justice, you say. What justice are you looking for in this old place?"

"Development plans. Are they housed here?"

"They are." She eyed me then looked at Benji. "I used to have one just like that. Bigger and a girl, but she had collie in her, too."

"Benji is the perfect mixture," I said.

The woman stopped to pat him then fished a set of keys from her pocket.

"If I promise not to breathe a word about you helping us, could you sneak us in?" I asked.

"And risk my job? Not likely."

"Please! It's about a recent murder. Emily Brewer."

That made her pause. "I know her aunt. I sometimes drink at the Harbour Arms."

I clasped my hands together. "That's my pub. Veronica Vale. I'm friends with Mabel."

"Oh! You're the lady boss."

I smiled. "Indeed, I am. And I want to help Mabel."

"By looking at development plans?"

"We'll be in and out as swiftly as possible."

She placed a key in the door. "I like Players and London dry gin. A big bottle."

My gaze narrowed. "I'm rather partial to a gin fizz, but where can I find a shop selling such items at this hour?"

"You own a pub, don't you?"

Oh, foolish Veronica. After getting her assurances the cigarettes and alcohol would give me access to the archives, I shot off with Benji. Luck was on our side, and the pub door was open, a delivery being taken in. I almost knocked Mabel off her feet as I whizzed in and behind the bar.

"What in the blue blazes are you doing up at this time?" Mabel had her dressing gown on, her hair still in curlers under a net.

"Sorry, no time to explain." I left money on the bar. "This is about Emily."

"What does my deceased niece need with a packet of Players and a bottle of gin?" Mabel asked.

I waved the cigarettes as I raced off, Benji thoroughly enjoying the pace, and headed back to the archive. As promised, we were let in by the cleaner and shown where the development plans were stored.

The cleaning lady left us to it, having already opened the gin and taken a sneaky sip.

Being used to the logical archival documenting system, I made swift work of locating the appropriate documents. I checked planning applications, council minutes, and newspaper articles.

I repeatedly glanced at Emily's notepad, flipped open to the correct page. "Development. Pollution. Fair rates," I murmured. Emily had seen the pieces of a puzzle, considered it irregular, and chased the story.

Benji rested his head on my knee, sensing my sadness as it settled over me when all the clues came together, and I knew exactly why Emily had been killed and by whom.

I gently ruffled his fur to soothe him. "It's time to gather the suspects and let Councillor Havisham go free from his murder charge."

It took almost three hours to gather everyone of note at the Harbour Arms. After I'd shown Jacob the new information, he'd taken no convincing as to who killed Emily and had dashed around like a young pup, not a man who'd almost been blown to pieces a short while ago.

Mabel nudged me as we waited by her bar inside the pub. She was no longer in her curlers and dressing gown, but instead wore an expression of surprise. "Can't you let me in on this? Emily was my niece."

"I don't want to scare off the killer," I said. "They have influence and could skip the country if we don't catch them in front of everybody."

Mabel huffed a breath. "What's she doing here?"

Lady Lizzie appeared in the doorway, looking as fresh as a daisy. Her gaze met mine, and she hurried over. "I received your note. I was most intrigued."

"As was I. I discovered the information you'll find of interest when looking into what happened to Emily." I kept my tone neutral, not wanting to give too much away.

"Of course. You deal with that first. How clever of you. But we must talk after this. I have a position for you. And I assure you, I'm an excellent employer."

I nodded demurely. In any other circumstance, I might be interested in working for such an influential woman. After catching Jacob's eye, I lifted my chin. Bishop appeared by the door with two officers, preventing any escape attempts. He gestured at me to take the lead, and I appreciated his confidence in me.

The rest of the assembled party, Councillor Havisham and Doctor Patterson, both in handcuffs, Tommy McAllister and Ivy Vance, looked on with a mixture of sternness and concern.

"I'll keep this brief, because I'd like to return to the holiday I was supposed to be having," I began.

"Some holiday," Tommy said. "You've been racing around Margate like the new rollercoaster."

"Indeed. This visit has been less than relaxing," I said. "As you all know, Emily Brewer recently died. At first, the police believed she fell, but it was quickly determined someone pushed her off the pier."

Mabel shook her head. "And whoever it was, shame on you."

Lady Lizzie raised a hand. "Do I need to be here for this part? I could step outside until you're free to conduct our business."

"Please, stay," I said. "At first, the finger of blame pointed at Tommy or Ivy. Tommy thought he could buy Emily off, but she came back, looking into suspicions of money laundering."

He shrugged. "She found nothing. No one ever will."

"Perhaps. And Ivy refused to help Emily when she asked for information."

Tommy glanced at Ivy. "Good girl. You know who looks after you."

She nodded and discreetly winked at Bishop.

"Was it them?" Doctor Patterson asked.

"They have alibis. Tommy was entertaining a lady friend, and Ivy was at a party," I said.

"I told you it wasn't me," Tommy said. "Honestly, you make a few mistakes when you're younger, and you're tarred for life."

"Well, it wasn't me!" Councillor Havisham blustered. "My reputation will be in tatters if anyone learns of my arrest."

"I'll get to you in a moment," I said. "Doctor Patterson has been peddling unprescribed medication to young people. Emily caught wind of his behaviour after a friend died. She confronted him."

Mabel took a step forward. "Did you do this to my niece?"

"No! I ... I may have made a few prescribing errors, but I'm no killer." Doctor Patterson gulped.

"The police think otherwise," I said. "Not for Emily, but for her friend, whose heart gave out on him. You're under investigation for that death, illegally selling medicine, and drugging your wife."

"I suppose he couldn't keep her satisfied," Tommy said with a smirk.

Doctor Patterson flushed bright red and stared at his shoes.

"And then we have the good councillor, grown fat on the money he took from hardworking men." I shook my head, still not over the shock of discovering how poorly Councillor Havisham had behaved.

"Steady on. There's competition for these waters. How else should I decide who receives a licence?" he spluttered.

"By doing your due diligence and not by the size of the envelope full of money given to you." I glanced at Bishop. He was still content to let me lead. "The police are interested in how widespread this corruption goes. You'll be staying with them and answering their questions until they're satisfied."

"The councilman didn't murder my Emily?" Mabel asked.

"Councillor Havisham was taking bribes in the harbour when Emily died," I said.

"Who does that leave us with?" Mabel's fierce glare went around the room as the group assessed each other.

I turned to Lady Lizzie. "Will you tell them, or should I?"

There was a pregnant pause as all eyes turned to Lady Lizzie. She gently cleared her throat. "There appears to have been a misunderstanding. Although I am interested in learning about what happened to Emily, I'm not involved. Miss Vale invited me to the Harbour Arms to discuss a business opportunity she discovered whilst researching the archives. As you all know, I endorse and invest in local commerce if it's of benefit to Margate."

"The note I sent to you was not strictly accurate, although I do want to discuss your business investments," I said. "Mabel provided me with Emily's source material for her stories. She discovered a final box of notepads, and the contents of one revealed Emily was investigating a story about unscrupulous development plans. Plans for private commerce led by you."

A flicker of uncertainty entered Lady Lizzie's eyes. "You're mistaken, as was Emily. We discussed this matter, and everything was ironed out. I only ever work for the benefit of Margate. I'm a charitable patron to many artistic endeavours, including funding Emily's journalism training."

"Something you must regret," Jacob said, "since Emily used those skills to uncover your secrets."

Lady Lizzie turned to the door, but seeing it blocked, focused back on me. "I don't like what you're suggesting."

"You probably like it about as much as Emily liked being pushed off the pier," I said. "We know she put up a fight. Her body was covered in bruises. I'm sure, if you allow it, an inspection of your arms and legs will reveal similar bruises and scrapes."

"My Emily would never go down without a fight," Mabel said. "And since she insisted on going out at all hours of the day and night, I made sure she knew how to look after herself."

"Maybe so, but you don't have my permission to inspect my limbs for marks that aren't there," Lady Lizzie said sternly. "This is an error, and I don't appreciate being lied to. I insist you let me leave."

"And I insist you tell us the truth," I said. "You've been buying private houses and parcels of land at rock-bottom prices, convincing the people who owned them they were worthless. Yes, on their own, they have little value, but the plans you submitted to the council show that, when you join up those buildings and the land, you have a substantial plot. A plot you plan on selling for an enormous profit."

"I don't go around submitting development plans," Lady Lizzie said. "I have people who do that for me. If there's any blame here, it's down to their incompetency, not mine."

"I spoke to some of your staff first thing this morning as soon as I finished my research in the archive," I said. "There was some reluctance, but when they realised the seriousness of the situation, they were quick to distance themselves from being involved in a murder."

"I had nothing to do with Emily's death," Lady Lizzie said. "You all know me. I adore Margate. I do what's best for it."

"To some extent, you do," I said. "But you think what's best for the town is taking land and buildings from simple folk, telling them you're giving them the best price, and then adding to your already substantial fortune. You wouldn't have passed the profits on to them, would you?"

"It's called business," Lady Lizzie said. "I broke no laws. I paid those people a fair rate. Most of their houses were beyond saving and needed to be condemned. Why shouldn't I reinvigorate the slum parts of Margate? It'll benefit everybody who lives here. Yes, I'll make a profit, but I was the only one with the forethought and intellect to do anything about it."

"Records of house and building purchases are available for public inspection," I said. "You paid those people a pittance. You most likely used your charm and influence to create a veneer of honesty. Emily discovered what you were up to and confronted you. Did she tell you to do the right thing? You wouldn't have liked being told what to do."

"Is this true?" Mabel asked. "Emily trusted you. She'd have been happy to meet you at any time. And I know you've met on the pier before."

"This is ridiculous. I was at my private beach home with friends. I went there after leaving the amusements."

"Is that the home that backs onto the beach?" Bishop asked.

"What of it?" Lady Lizzie enquired.

"You have private steps leading onto the beach," Bishop said. "It would have been easy to slip out for ten minutes to meet Emily. The pier is close to your home."

Lady Lizzie huffed out a breath. "This is nonsense. I demand you check with my guests. They're all staying for the week. Let me speak to them, and they will vouch for me."

"We have police officers at your home now," I said.

Her face paled. "Well, perhaps I stepped out to take some fresh air. It had been a hectic evening. That's not a crime, is it?"

"It's a crime if that fresh air took you to the pier, where you'd arranged to meet Emily," I said. "One of Emily's finest qualities was that she never backed down when she saw an injustice. What you were attempting was wrong, and she wanted you to stop or she'd expose you. It would have tarnished your good name."

"And as you're often overheard saying, your family's reputation means everything to you," Bishop said.

Lady Lizzie drew in a steadying breath. "I'm appalled by these accusations. I insist on contacting my lawyer. He'll get you to see sense."

"You can make that telephone call at the police station," Bishop said. "Lady Lizzie, you're under arrest for Emily Brewer's murder."

Ruby stepped from foot to foot. She wore a simple white dress and held a bunch of daisies. She'd been staring at the entrance to the registry office for ten minutes, barely breathing, her expression tight.

I stood beside Jacob, my mother, and Matthew next to me, Benji and Felix settled by our feet. My stomach was churning, so I could only imagine how dreadful Ruby felt. Her marriage ceremony to Alfonso was supposed to have started fifteen minutes ago, and he had yet to make an appearance.

I glanced at Ruby again, but she'd refused to meet my eye since we'd arrived at the registry office. Things were frosty between us, but I desperately wanted to comfort my best friend.

"We should do something," my mother whispered to me. "Matthew, go outside and see where Alfonso is. Maybe he has cold feet and is lurking by the door. He could just need a nudge to come inside."

Matthew grimaced, but he caught hold of Felix's lead and headed to the door, peeking around it. He looked back and shook his head.

"He'll be here!" Ruby said. "Alfonso has dreadful timekeeping. It's one of the things I planned to work on once we were wed."

"Is there anything he needed to do this morning before you got married?" I asked.

"He'll be here," Ruby repeated. "I don't know what all the fuss is about."

The registrar, who'd been patiently waiting at the front of the small room, cleared his throat. "We do have another wedding in fifteen minutes. If your groom is not here soon—"

"Alfonso will arrive," Ruby said. "And when he does, you'll just have to speak quickly, so we get through our vows. He wants to marry me. He promised me last night it was all he'd been thinking about."

"He was most likely thinking about what a mistake he'd made," Jacob muttered to me. "He must have thought Ruby's talk about marriage was just her getting caught up in a holiday romance."

"Alfonso proposed to her," I whispered back. "Ruby pushed nothing on the man."

"Then he got caught up in the romance, too," Jacob said. "What are we going to do?"

I longed to comfort Ruby, but any words would be taken the wrong way. I nudged Benji towards her. He was an astute dog and picked up on heightened emotions, so he quickly went to her side. He leaned against Ruby's leg and gently whined. She reached down and absently patted him, still looking at the door.

Five more minutes passed, and Alfonso was nowhere to be seen.

Matthew slid from his seat and joined Ruby at the front. "Any man who makes you wait this long is wrong for you."

Surprised by Matthew's boldness, I sat there in mute shock.

Ruby slid him a glance, and there were tears sparkling in her eyes. "It was one of the things I didn't like about him. I even said I'd buy him a watch if his timekeeping didn't improve."

"Your perfect man will always be by your side, not making you stand alone, feeling unloved," Matthew said. "Ruby, you're cracking. You're smart, funny, love horses and dogs. You always look out for my sister when she gets herself into one scrape or another. And you're pretty to boot. If this fool can't see what he's got, then it's his loss."

Ruby looked away, her blinking rapid. "I ... I don't know what to do. Why isn't Alfonso here?"

Matthew touched her arm. "I say, we get out of here and enjoy some fish and chips on the beach."

The registrar shuffled his feet. "I'm afraid your time is up. My next couple is outside."

Ruby gulped several times, failing to stop a tear from trickling down her cheek. "He told me he loved me. We were to honeymoon in Italy. I was to meet his family, and they'd welcome me with open arms. What am I supposed to do now?"

"Go back to the life you love," Matthew said. "Be your usual wild, free, fun-loving self. And when the right man comes along, you'll know it. I know it's not this one."

Ruby sniffed back more tears. "I don't suppose you want to get married, do you? When you're not hiding in your bedroom in your unwashed pyjamas, you're very sweet. And when you have a bath, you scrub up well."

Matthew's chuckle was awkward. "You're like a sister to me."

"Oh! Yes. Point taken. It wouldn't be a romantic relationship, would it? And one does need a little romance in one's life." Ruby glanced at me. "At least, most of us do."

"She's still angry at you," Jacob whispered.

"I'll take as much of that anger as needed," I replied. Ruby's heart had been wounded, and if I had to take the brunt of her irritation until she was healed, then so be it. That's what best friends did for each other.

Ruby tossed her daisies at the registrar. "Give these to your next bride. I have no use for them. And if that Italian scoundrel dares to show his face, tell him I never want to see him again." She stomped along the short aisle and out of the door without a backward glance. Matthew dashed after her with Felix, my mother not far behind.

I hurried after Ruby, but Jacob caught hold of my elbow. "Let Matthew and your mother take care of her for once. Between them, they'll smother her in affection, and she'll have forgotten all about that fool of a man by the end of the day."

I sighed as I called Benji to my side. "You have a point. My brother has a tender heart. And while he's focusing on other people's problems, he's not so worried about his own issues. The same goes for my mother. She won't even think about her sore feet while she's caring for Ruby."

"Good. And I'm glad we finally have a moment to ourselves with no mysteries to get in our way." He drew in a breath. "Because there's something I've been meaning to talk to you about."

My heart skipped a beat. I couldn't avoid this conversation anymore. "Is it romance? Because if it is, you can see how badly things have turned out for Ruby. It's too scary a topic to consider."

"Romance? Well, that's on my mind, but I thought things were rubbing along nicely between us. You're happy, aren't you? You said you wanted to take things at a slow pace, and I'm happy to wait. Especially with my leg, I'm up to nothing more than a gentle walk and hand-holding."

I blushed as I realised what he was talking about. "Oh! I'm in no hurry either. And yes, I'm happy. I'm almost sorry I waited so long before letting my feelings show."

Jacob chuckled. "As much as you do let them show. But I'm not complaining. I know your character, and that's one of the many things I adore about you."

I took a breath, watching my family surround Ruby with all the love and attention she needed as we walked behind them towards the fish and chip shop. "If you don't want to talk about our relationship, then what's on your mind?"

"It's something I've been trying to tell you ever since we got here," Jacob said. "I thought you'd need time to let the information sink in, and I didn't want you to rush off on a new investigation when I was unable to assist. Well, it's an old investigation, actually."

"Go on. Are you talking about one of the cold cases you've been looking into?" My interest was piqued. When Jacob had been recovering after his altercation with an unexploded bomb, one of his colleagues supplied him with a number of cold cases to review. Had he found new information that could lead to a conviction?

Jacob looked straight ahead, his jaw tight. "When Sergeant Matthers brought me those old files, I didn't pay much attention to them at first. But I got so bored that I started reading through the notes. Most of the information was no use, but one case stood out to me. And I promised myself, when I got out of the hospital, I'd take a proper look at it."

"And you've found new evidence? How exciting! Perhaps this could be our first official case," I said. "Where did the crime take place?"

"A long way from here." Jacob stopped walking and turned to me, grasping hold of my hand. "Veronica, one of those cold cases had details of your father's death in it."

I was so shocked, I couldn't speak, just let my mouth hang open.

Jacob hesitated, indecision flickering across his face. "I've looked through the information, and I've even made a few telephone calls."

I cleared my throat to loosen the tight band threatening to throttle me. "And what did those conversations reveal?"

Jacob's grip tightened. "I don't think your father ended his own life. I think he was murdered."

Historical notes

The Harbour Arms

While researching locations for the book, I merged two seaside sites in Kent. Margate and Folkestone.

I briefly lived in the modern-day Folkestone during Covid, so I had few opportunities to explore, but I regularly walked along the empty Harbour Arms and looked out at the sea.

The 19th-century harbour focused on ferry boats, industry, and steamers, taking people abroad. The construction of a new pier took place in stages over the decades and was completed in 1904.

The area played a key role throughout the Great War, with troops passing through the port and post sent to and from the Western Front. 8.6 million passengers passed through the port between 1914 to 1918, including troops heading to France or returning home on leave.

In the summer of 1915 a buffet, called the Mole Café, was set up on the Harbour Arm, offering free tea and refreshments to soldiers sailors, and the Red Cross. Volunteers ran this service, and two local ladies, Margaret Ann and Florence Augusta Jeffery, were awarded the Order of the British Empire, the Queen Elisabeth Medal, and the Medal of Gratitude.

Margate Pier (where the murder occurred)

The pier was initially made of wood and built in 1824. It was rebuilt in iron in 1855 and extended and added to. It closed in 1976 over safety concerns and was damaged in a storm two years later. It was eventually demolished.

The original pier was 1,100 feet (340 m.) It was known as the Jarvis Landing Stage and allowed ships to load and unload passengers at low tide.

After the wooden pier was storm-damaged in 1851, a new iron pier was erected in 1853. It became the first iron seaside pier in the world. A pavilion was built at the pierhead in 1858 and used as a station building for steamship departures and arrivals.

The pier was extended and an octagonal pierhead added. There was drama in 1877 when the pier was cut through by a shipwreck during a storm, and fifty people were trapped on the seaward side until the next day when they could be rescued!

Over the years, the pier continued to be damaged, until a storm surge in 1978 destroyed most of it, and ended the possibility of a new pier, due to cost constraints. The local museum in Margate displays some of the remnants that were washed up on the beach.

Margate and Folkestone today

Sadly, like many British seaside towns that relied on tourism to bolster their income, they're a shadow of their former selves. And if you had a choice, would you swim in the murky waters of the English Channel or the North Sea, or the warmer, clearer Mediterranean?

In the 1960s, cheap foreign package holidays flourished, and people abandoned the often chilly English seaside for clear blue waters and guaranteed sunshine.

Both towns declined and still suffer today, with issues around poorly paid jobs, high numbers of unemployed, and a general air of neglect when you wander the streets. There are still some gems to be found in these towns, but the struggle is apparent.

Also by

Death at the Fireside Inn
Death at the Drunken Duck
Death at the Craven Arms
Death at the Dripping Tap
Death at the Harbour Arms
Death at the Swan Tavern

More mysteries coming soon. While you wait, why not investigate K.E. O'Connor's back catalogue (Kitty's alter ego.)

About the author

Immerse yourself into Kitty Kildare's cleverly woven historical British mysteries. Follow the mystery in the Veronica Vale Investigates series and enjoy the dazzle and delights of 1920s England.

Kitty is a not-so-secret pen name of established cozy mystery author K.E.O'Connor, who decided she wanted to time travel rather than cast spells! Enjoy the twists and turns.

Join in the fun and get Kitty's newsletter (and secret wartime files about our sleuthing ladies!)

Newsletter: https://BookHip.com/JJPKDLB
Website: www.kittykildare.com
Facebook: www.facebook.com/kittykildare